Praise for *The Good*

'An amazing adventure story, told with sparkling style and sleight of hand'

Jacqueline Wilson

'A total showstopper of a story. Rundell's finest yet'

Emma Carroll

'A new Katherine Rundell book is always an event, but this is another triumph and then some. A wickedly exciting heist with heart'

Kiran Millwood Hargrave

'Likely to be the best children's book you'll read this year'

The Times

'Captivating … every inch of it is a delight'

Sunday Times

Praise for *The Explorer*

'A wildly exciting adventure … One of our most talented writers for children'

Observer

'Katherine Rundell is now unarguably in the first rank'

Philip Pullman

'Reading this delicious book is like eating electricity'

Sunday Times, Children's Book of the Year

'One of the most captivating books of the year'

Spectator

'An adventure story to die for ... What a discovery'

The Times

'I cannot imagine the child who wouldn't be delighted by it'

Independent

Praise for *The Wolf Wilder*

'A triumph! Exciting, moving, highly original, fierce, completely convincing'

Philip Pullman

'The most exciting new children's novel for a decade'

Independent

'The kind of novel that reminds you why books are worth reading and life is worth living'

Lauren St John

'A Fabergé egg of a novel – rich, bright and perfect'

Robin Stevens

ROOFTOPPERS

Books by Katherine Rundell

The Girl Savage

Rooftoppers

The Wolf Wilder

The Explorer

The Good Thieves

For younger readers

One Christmas Wish

For adult readers

Why You Should Read Children's Books,
Even Though You Are So Old and Wise

KATHERINE
RUNDELL

Illustrated
by
MARIE-ALICE HAREL

BLOOMSBURY
CHILDREN'S BOOKS
LONDON OXFORD NEW YORK NEW DELHI SYDNEY

BLOOMSBURY CHILDREN'S BOOKS
Bloomsbury Publishing Plc
50 Bedford Square, London WC1B 3DP, UK

BLOOMSBURY, BLOOMSBURY CHILDREN'S BOOKS and the Diana logo
are trademarks of Bloomsbury Publishing Plc

First published in Great Britain in 2013 by Faber and Faber Limited
This edition published in Great Britain in 2020 by Bloomsbury Publishing Plc

A catalogue record for this book is available from the British Library

ISBN: PB: 978-1-5266-2480-2; eBook: 978-1-5266-2479-6

6 8 10 9 7 5

Typeset by Westchester Publishing Services

Printed and bound in Great Britain by CPI Group (UK) Ltd, Croydon CR0 4YY

To my brother, with love

INTRODUCTION

The idea for *Rooftoppers* came, without warning, while I was on a rooftop. When I was twenty-one I became a Fellow of All Souls College in Oxford, which was founded in 1438: a building with tall towers and some very stern-looking gargoyles. I have always loved to climb – trees and rocks and occasionally drainpipes – and when I first arrived there, I found out about a secret trapdoor that could take you, with a jump and a scramble, up on to the roof. I was up there climbing among the gargoyles one night (it had to be dark, as it's technically very illegal) when I found a dusty old beer bottle in the corner by the parapet. It made me wonder: what if somebody had

been living up here, close to the sky, and we didn't know?

That's how it began: with a *what if*. So many stories have a *what if* at their core: What if you had a scar on your forehead and had to save the world from an evil wizard? What if you went through a wardrobe and on the other side there was unfathomable beauty – and snow, and a witch, and a lion? What then? What would happen next? What if there really were people living up on the rooftop of an old college? What if there were people living secret rooftop lives all over the world? *What if?*

I have always loved being up high; I love aeroplanes, and mountains, and flying on the flying trapeze. I've always been shy, and I love the idea of seeing the world when it can't see you. When I was younger, I taught myself to walk on a tightrope – I find the feeling of focus and balance and height it brings a miraculous thing. I practised for many years (breaking only a couple of toes in the process) and can now walk a wire backwards and forwards, and in high-heeled shoes. (This is not, alas, a particularly

useful skill in the real world.) So I knew I wanted *Rooftoppers* to have a tightrope-walking boy in it: somebody who made it look as if gravity didn't apply to him.

Most of all, I wanted *Rooftoppers* to be about recklessly, riotously brave people – because I think, both in real life and fiction, they do us all a service: there is so much optimism and hope in their daring that it spreads out into the world around them. I wanted to write a book about children's brilliance and boldness, about children who charge across the rooftops of Paris, leaping and somersaulting, searching, hunting. I wanted to write an adventure story that would make the children who read it want to go on an adventure: a book that would say we should never ignore a possible.

Katherine Rundell, March 2020

CHAPTER ONE

On the morning of its first birthday, a baby was found floating in a cello case in the middle of the English Channel.

It was the only living thing for miles. Just the baby, and some dining-room chairs, and the tip of a ship disappearing into the ocean. There had been music in the dining hall, and it was music so loud and so good that nobody had noticed the water flooding in over the carpet. The violins went on sawing for some time after the screaming had begun. Sometimes the shriek of a passenger would duet with a high C.

The baby was found wrapped for warmth in the

musical score of a Beethoven symphony. It had drifted almost a mile from the ship, and was the last to be rescued. The man who lifted it into the rescue boat was a fellow passenger, and a scholar. It is a scholar's job to notice things. He noticed that it was a girl, with hair the colour of lightning, and the smile of a shy person.

Think of night-time with a speaking voice. Or think how moonlight might talk, or think of ink, if ink had vocal cords. Give those things a narrow aristocratic face with hooked eyebrows, and long arms and legs, and that is what the baby saw as she was lifted out of her cello case and up into safety. His name was Charles Maxim, and he determined, as he held her in his large hands – at arm's length, as he would a leaky flowerpot – that he would keep her.

The baby was almost certainly one year old. They knew this because of the red rosette pinned to her front, which read, '1!'

'Or rather,' said Charles Maxim, 'the child is either one year old, or she has come first in a competition. I believe babies are rarely keen participants in competitive sport. Shall we therefore assume it is the former?' The girl held on to his earlobe with a grubby finger and thumb. 'Happy birthday, my child,' he said.

Charles did not only give the baby a birthday. He also gave her a name. He chose Sophie, on that first day, on the grounds that nobody could possibly object to it. 'Your day has been dramatic and extraordinary enough, child,' he said. 'It might be best to have the most ordinary name available. You can be Mary, or Betty, or Sophie. Or, at a stretch, Mildred. Your choice.' Sophie had smiled when he said 'Sophie', so Sophie it was. Then he fetched his coat, and folded her up in it, and took her home in a carriage. It rained a little, but it did not worry either of them. Charles did not generally notice the weather, and Sophie had already survived a lot of water that day.

Charles had never really known a child before. He told Sophie as much on the way home: 'I do, I'm afraid, understand books far more readily than I understand people. Books are so easy to get along with.' The carriage ride took four hours; Charles held Sophie on the very edge of his knee, and told her about himself, as though she were an acquaintance at a tea party. He was thirty-six years old, and six foot three. He spoke English to people and French to cats, and Latin to the birds. He had once nearly killed himself trying to read and ride a horse at the same time. 'But I will be more careful,' he said, 'now that there is you, little cello child.' Charles's home was beautiful, but it was not safe; it was all staircases and slippery floorboards and sharp corners. 'I'll buy some smaller chairs,' he said. 'And we'll have thick red carpets! Although – how does one go about acquiring carpets? I don't suppose you know, Sophie?'

Unsurprisingly, Sophie did not answer. She was too young to talk; and she was asleep.

She woke when they drew up in a street smelling of trees and horse dung. Sophie loved the house at first

sight. The bricks were painted the brightest white in London, and shone even in the dark. The basement was used to store the overflow of books and paintings and several brands of spiders; and the roof belonged to the birds. Charles lived in the space in between.

At home, after a hot bath in front of the stove, Sophie looked very white and fragile. Charles had not known that a baby was so terrifyingly tiny a thing. She felt too small in his arms. He was almost relieved when there was a knock at the door; he laid Sophie down carefully on a chair, with a Shakespearean play as a booster seat, and went up the stairs two at a time.

When he returned, he was accompanied by a large grey-haired woman; *Hamlet* was slightly damp, and Sophie was looking embarrassed. Charles scooped her up, and set her down – hesitating first over an umbrella stand in a corner, and then the top of the stove – inside the sink. He smiled, and his eyebrows and eyes smiled too. 'Please don't worry,' he said. 'We all have accidents, Sophie.' Then he bowed at the woman. 'Let me introduce you. Sophie, this is Miss Eliot, from the National

Childcare Agency. Miss Eliot, this is Sophie, from the ocean.'

The woman sighed – an official sort of sigh, it would have sounded, from Sophie's place in the sink – and frowned, and pulled clean clothes from a parcel. 'Give her to me.'

Charles took the clothes from her. 'I took this child from the sea, madam.' Sophie watched, with large eyes. 'She has nobody to keep her safe. Whether I like it or not, she is my responsibility.'

'Not forever.'

'I beg your pardon?'

'The child is your *ward*. She is not your daughter.' This was the sort of woman who spoke in italics. You would be willing to lay bets that her hobby was organising people. 'This is a temporary arrangement.'

'I beg to differ,' said Charles. 'But we can fight about that later. The child is cold.' He handed the vest to Sophie, who sucked on it. He took it back and put it on for her. Then he hefted her in his arms, as though about to guess her weight at a fair, and looked at her

closely. 'You see? She seems a very intelligent baby.' Sophie's fingers, he saw, were long and thin, and clever. 'And she has hair the colour of lightning. How could you possibly resist her?'

'I'll have to come round, to check on her, and I really don't have the time to spare. *A man can't do this kind of thing alone.*'

'Certainly, please do come,' said Charles – and he added, as if he couldn't stop himself, 'if you feel that you absolutely can't stay away. I will endeavour to be grateful. But this child is my responsibility. Do you understand?'

'But it's a *child*! You're a *man*!'

'Your powers of observation are formidable,' said Charles. 'You are a credit to your optician.'

'But what are you going to *do* with her?'

Charles looked bewildered. 'I am going to love her. That should be enough, if the poetry I've read is anything to go by.' Charles handed Sophie a red apple; then took it back, and rubbed it on his sleeve until he could see his face in it. He said, 'I am sure the secrets

of childcare, dark and mysterious though they no doubt are, are not impenetrable.'

Charles set the baby on his knee, handed her the apple, and began to read out loud to her from *A Midsummer Night's Dream*.

It was not, perhaps, the perfect way to begin a new life, but it showed potential.

CHAPTER TWO

There was, in the offices of the National Childcare Agency in Westminster, a cabinet; and in the cabinet, a red file marked 'Guardians: Character Assessment'. In the red file, there was a smaller blue file marked 'Maxim, Charles'. It read, 'C.P. Maxim is bookish, as one would expect of a scholar: also apparently generous, awkward, industrious. He is unusually tall but doctor's reports suggest he is otherwise healthy. He is stubbornly certain of his ability to care for a female ward.'

Perhaps such things are contagious, because Sophie grew up tall and generous and bookish and awkward.

By the time she turned seven, she had legs as long and thin as golf umbrellas, and a collection of stubborn certainties.

For her seventh birthday, Charles baked a chocolate cake. It was not an absolute success, because it had sagged in the middle, but Sophie declared loyally that that was her favourite kind of cake. 'Because,' she said, 'the dip leaves room for more icing. I like my icing to be extragavant.'

'I am glad to hear it,' said Charles. 'Although the word is traditionally pronounced *extravagant*, I believe. Happy probably seventh birthday, dear heart. How about a little birthday Shakespeare?'

Sophie had a habit of breaking plates, and so they had been eating their cake off the front cover of *A Midsummer Night's Dream*. Now Charles wiped it on his sleeve, and opened at the middle. 'Will you read me some Titania?'

Sophie made a face. 'I'd rather be Puck.' She tried a few lines, but it was slow going. She waited until Charles was looking away, then dropped the book on the floor and did a handstand on it.

Charles laughed. 'Bravo!' He applauded against the table. 'You look the stuff that elves are made of.'

Sophie fell over into the kitchen table, stood up, and tried again against the door.

'Wonderful! You're getting better; almost perfect.'

'Only almost?' Sophie wobbled, and squinted at him upside down. Her eyeballs were starting to burn, but she stayed where she was. 'Aren't my legs straight?'

'Almost. Your left knee looks a little uncertain. Anyway, no human is perfect. Nobody since Shakespeare.'

Sophie thought about that later, in bed. 'No human is perfect,' Charles had said, but he was wrong. Charles was perfect. Charles had hair the same colour as the banister, and eyes that had magic in them. He had

inherited his house and all his clothes from his father. They had once been beautiful, razzle-dazzle Savile Row one-hundred-per-cent silk, and were now fifty per cent silk, fifty per cent hole. Charles had no musical instruments, but he sang to her; and when Sophie was elsewhere, he sang to the birds, and to the woodlice that occasionally invaded the kitchen. His voice was pitch-perfect. It sounded like flying.

Sometimes the feeling of the sinking ship would come back to Sophie, in the middle of the night, and then she found that she needed desperately to climb things. Climbing was the only thing that made her feel safe. Charles allowed her to sleep on top of the wardrobe. He slept on the floor beneath her, just in case.

Sophie didn't entirely understand him. Charles ate little, and slept rarely, and he did not smile as often as other people. But he had kindness where other people had lungs, and politeness in his fingertips. If, when reading and walking at the same time, he bumped into a lamp post, he would apologise and check that the lamp post was unhurt.

One morning a week, Miss Eliot came to the house,

'to sort out any problems'. (Sophie could have said, 'what problems?' but she soon learned to stay silent.) Miss Eliot would look around the house, which was peeling at the corners, and at the spiderwebs in the empty larder, and she would shake her head.

'What do you *eat*?'

It was true that food was more interesting in their house than in the homes of Sophie's friends. Sometimes Charles forgot about meat for months at a time. Clean plates seemed to break whenever Sophie came near them, and so he served roast potato chips on atlases of the world, spread open at the map of Hungary. In fact he would have been happy to live on biscuits, and tea, and whisky at bedtime. When Sophie first learned to read, Charles had kept the whisky in a bottle labelled 'cat's urine', so that Sophie would not touch it, but she had uncorked the bottle, and sipped it, and then sniffed at the underside of the cat next door. They were not at all similar, though equally unpleasant.

'We have bread,' said Sophie. 'And fish in tins.'

'You have *what*?' said Miss Eliot.

'I like fish in tins,' said Sophie. 'And we have ham.'

'Do you? I've never seen a single slice of ham in this place.'

'Every day! Or,' she added, because Sophie was more honest than she found convenient, 'definitely sometimes. And cheese. And apples. And I drink a whole pint of milk for breakfast.'

'But how can Charles let you *live* like that? I don't think this can be good for a child. It's not *right*.'

They managed, in fact, very well, but Miss Eliot never quite understood. When Miss Eliot said 'right', Sophie thought, she meant 'neat'. Sophie and Charles did not live neatly, but neatness, Sophie thought, was not necessary for happiness.

'The thing is, Miss Eliot,' said Sophie, 'the thing is, I don't have the sort of face that ever looks neat. Charles says I have untidy eyes. Because of the fleck, you see.' Sophie's skin was too pale, and it showed blotches in the cold, and her hair had never, in her memory, been without knots. Sophie did not mind, though; because in her memory of her mother she saw the same sort of hair and skin: and her mother, she felt

sure, was beautiful. Her mother, she was sure, had smelt of cool air and soot, and had worn trousers with patches at the ankle.

The trousers, in fact, were perhaps the beginning of the troubles. When Sophie was nearing eight years old, she asked Charles for a pair of trousers.

'Trousers? Is that not rather unusual for women?'

'No,' said Sophie. 'I don't think so. My mother wears them.'

'*Wore* them, Sophie, my child.'

'*Wears* them. Black ones. But I'd like mine to be red.'

'Um. You wouldn't prefer a skirt?' He looked worried.

Sophie made a face. 'No, I really do want trousers. Please.'

There were no trousers in the shops that would fit her, only the grey shorts that boys wore – and, 'Good heavens!' said Charles. 'You look like a maths lesson' – so Charles sewed four pairs himself in brightly coloured cotton and gave them to her wrapped in newspaper. One of them had one leg longer than

the other. Sophie loved them. Miss Eliot was shocked; and '*Girls*,' she said, 'don't wear trousers.' But Sophie insisted that they did.

'My mother wore trousers. I know she did. She used to dance in them, when she played her cello.'

'She can't have,' said Miss Eliot. It was always the same. 'Women do not play the cello, Sophie. And you were *much* too young to remember. You must try to be more honest, Sophie.'

'But she did. The trousers were black, and greyish at the knee. And she wore black shoes. I remember.'

'You are imagining things, my dear.' Miss Eliot's voice was like a window slamming shut.

'But I promise, I'm *not*.'

'Sophie –'

'I'm not!' Sophie did not add, 'you potato-faced old hag!' but she did very much want to. The problem was that a person could not grow up with Charles without becoming polite to their very bones. To be impolite felt, to Sophie, like wearing dirty underwear, but it was difficult to be polite when people talked about her

mother. They were so very certain that she was making it up; and she was so very certain that they were wrong.

'Toenail eyes!' whispered Sophie. 'Buzzard! I *do* remember.' She felt a little better.

Sophie did remember her mother, in fact, clear and sharp. She did not remember a father; but she remembered a swirl of hair, and two thin cloth-covered legs kicking to the beat of wonderful music, and that wouldn't have been possible if the legs had been covered in skirt.

Sophie was also sure she remembered, very clearly, seeing her mother clinging to a floating door in the middle of the Channel.

Everybody said, 'A baby is too young to remember.' They said, 'You are remembering what you wish was true.' She grew sick of hearing it. But Sophie remembered seeing her mother wave for help. She had heard her mother whistle. Whistles are very distinctive. No matter what the police said, then, she knew her mother had not gone down inside the ship. Sophie was stubbornly certain.

Sophie whispered to herself in the dark every night: *My mother is still alive, and she is going to come for me one day.*

'She'll come for me,' said Sophie to Charles.

Charles would shake his head. 'That is almost impossible, dear heart.'

'*Almost* impossible means still possible.' Sophie tried to stand up straight and sound adult; people believed you more easily if you were taller. 'You always say, never ignore a possible.'

'But my child, it is so profoundly improbable, that it's not worth building a life on. It would be like trying to build a house on the back of a dragonfly.'

'She'll come for me,' said Sophie to Miss Eliot.

Miss Eliot was more blunt. 'Your mother is dead. No women survived,' she said. 'You mustn't allow yourself to get carried away.'

Sometimes it seemed difficult for the adults in Sophie's life to tell between 'carried away' and 'absolutely correct but unbelieved'. Sophie felt herself flushing. 'She will come,' she said. 'Or I'll go to her.'

'No, Sophie. That is not how the world works.' Miss

Eliot was sure that Sophie was mistaken, but then Miss Eliot was also sure that cross-stitch was *vital*, and Charles was *impossible*, which just showed that adults weren't always right.

One day Sophie found some red paint and wrote the name of the ship, *the Queen Mary*, and the date of the storm, on the white wall of the house; just in case her mother passed by.

Charles's face, when he found her, was too complicated for her to look at. But he helped her reach the high parts, and wash the brushes afterwards.

'A case,' he said to Miss Eliot, 'of the just in cases.'

'But she's –'

'She is only doing as I have told her.'

'You told her to vandalise your own house?'

'No. I have told her not to ignore life's possibles.'

CHAPTER THREE

Miss Eliot did not approve of Charles, nor of Sophie. She disliked Charles's carelessness with money, and his lateness at dinner.

She disliked Sophie's watching, listening face. 'It's not natural, in a little girl!' She hated their joint habit of writing each other notes on the wallpaper in the hall.

'It's not normal!' she said, scribbling on her notepad. 'It's not healthy!'

'On the contrary,' said Charles. 'The more words in a house the better, Miss Eliot.'

Miss Eliot also disliked Charles's hands, which were

inky, and his hat, which was coming adrift round the brim. She disapproved of Sophie's clothes.

Charles was not good at shopping. He spent a day standing, bewildered, in the middle of Bond Street, and came back with a parcel of boys' shirts. Miss Eliot was livid.

'You cannot let her wear that,' she said. 'People will think she is deranged.'

Sophie looked down at herself. She fingered the material. It felt quite normal to her; still a little stiff from the shop, but otherwise fine. 'How can you tell it's not a girl's shirt?' she asked.

'Boys' shirts button left over right. Blouses – please note, the word is *blouses* – button right over left. I am shocked that you don't know that.'

Charles put down the newspaper behind which he

had retreated. 'You are shocked that she doesn't know about *buttons*? Buttons are rarely key players in international affairs.'

'I beg your pardon?'

'I meant, she knows the things which are important. Not all of them, of course; she is still a child. But many.'

Miss Eliot sniffed. 'You'll forgive me; I may be old-fashioned, but I think buttons *do* matter.'

'Sophie,' said Charles, 'knows all the capitals of all the countries of the world.'

Sophie, standing in the doorway, whispered, '*Almost*.'

'She knows how to read, and how to draw. She knows the difference between a tortoise and a turtle. She knows one tree from another, and how to climb them. Only this morning she was telling me what is the collective noun for toads.'

'A knot,' said Sophie. 'It's a knot of toads.'

'And she whistles. You would have to be extraordinarily unintelligent not to see that Sophie's whistling is unusual. Extraordinarily unintelligent, or deaf.'

Charles might just as well not have spoken. Miss Eliot swept him aside with a single flick of her fingers.

'She'll need new shirts, please, Mr Maxim. *Women's* shirts. And, my lord, those trousers!'

Sophie didn't see the problem. Trousers were just skirts with extra sewing. 'I need them,' she said. 'Please let me keep them. You can't climb in a skirt. Or, you can, but then everyone would see your pants, and surely that would be worse?'

Miss Eliot frowned. She was not the sort of person who admitted to wearing pants.

'We'll let it pass for now. You're still a child. But this can't go on forever.'

'What? Why not?' Sophie touched the bookcase with her fingertips for luck. 'Yes, it can. Why wouldn't it?'

'It certainly can't. England is no place for untrained women.'

Above all, Miss Eliot disliked Charles's wish to take Sophie on sudden expeditions. London was dirty, she said, and Sophie would catch germs and bad habits.

On the day of Sophie's probably ninth birthday, Charles stood her on a chair and polished her shoes, while she ate toast with one hand and read a book with

the other. She turned the pages with her teeth. Crumbs and spit coated the corners of the paper but it was otherwise a satisfactory arrangement.

They were almost ready to leave the house for the concert hall when Miss Eliot stormed in.

'You can't take her out like that! She's filthy! And don't slouch, Sophie.'

Charles looked with interest at the top of Sophie's head. 'Is she?'

'Mr Maxim!' barked Miss Eliot. 'The girl has jam all down her top!'

'So she does.' Charles looked at Miss Eliot with courteous bewilderment. 'Does it matter?' Then, seeing Miss Eliot's hand reach towards her clipboard, he took a cloth and sponged at Sophie; as gently as if she were a painting.

Miss Eliot sniffed. 'There's some on the sleeve, too.'

'The rain will wash the rest off, surely? It's her birthday.'

'Dirt still applies on birthdays! You're not taking her to a zoo.'

'I see. Would you rather I took her to the zoo?' Charles tipped his head to one side. He looked, Sophie thought, like a particularly well-mannered panther. 'It may not be too late to change the tickets.'

'That isn't what I meant! She'll disgrace you. I would be embarrassed to be seen with her.'

Charles looked at Miss Eliot. Miss Eliot's eyes dropped first.

'She has shining shoes and shining eyes,' said Charles. 'That is smartness enough.' He handed Sophie the tickets to hold on to. 'Happy birthday, my child.' He kissed her forehead – the once-yearly birthday kiss – and helped Sophie from her chair.

There are many ways, Sophie knew, of helping people from their chairs. It is a very revealing thing to do. Miss Eliot, for instance, would prod you off with a wooden spoon. Charles did it carefully, by the fingertips, as though they were dancing – and he whistled the string section from *Così fan tutte* all the way down the street.

'Music, Sophie! Music is mad and wonderful.'

'Yes!' Charles had kept her birthday plans a secret, but his excitement was contagious. She skipped alongside him. 'What kind of music will it be?'

'Classical, Sophie.' His face was alight with happiness and his fingers were twitching at the tip. 'Clever, complicated music.'

'Oh. That's … wonderful.' Sophie was an unpractised liar. 'That will be so good.' In fact, Sophie thought, she *would* rather have gone to the zoo. Sophie had heard almost no classical music, and she would have been quite happy to keep it that way. She liked folk songs, and music you could dance to; very few just-turned-nine-year-olds, she imagined, could have said they liked classical music without lying a little.

The performance did not, as far as Sophie was concerned, start promisingly. The piano piece was long. The pianist had a moustache, and made the sorts of faces that Sophie associated with being very itchy.

'Charles?' Sophie glanced at Charles, and saw his lips were slightly open, and curved upwards in an expression of very listening happiness.

'Charles?'

'Yes, Sophie? And you must try to whisper.'

'Charles, how long does it go on for? I mean, it's not that it's not wonderful.' Sophie crossed her fingers behind her back. 'It's just that I ... wondered.'

'Only an hour, my child, alas. I could live here, in this seat, couldn't you?'

'Oh. An *hour*?' Sophie tried to sit still, but it was difficult. She sucked the end of her plait. She curled and uncurled her toes. She resolved, unsuccessfully, not to bite her thumbnail. She was at last on the borderland of sleep when three violins, a cello and a viola came on stage, accompanied by their musicians.

When they began to play, the music was different. It was sweeter, and wilder. Sophie sat up properly, and shifted forwards until only half an inch of her bottom was on her seat. It was so beautiful that it was difficult to breathe. If music can shine, Sophie thought, this music shone. It was like all the voices in all the choirs in the city rolled into a single melody. Her chest felt oddly swollen.

'It's like eight thousand birds, Charles! Charles! Isn't it like eight thousand birds?'

'Yes! But shhh, Sophie.'

The melody quickened, and Sophie's pulse kept time. It sounded at once familiar and new. It plucked at her fingers and feet.

Sophie's legs wouldn't stay still. She knelt up on her seat. After a moment, she risked a whisper. 'Charles! Listen! The cello sings, Charles!'

When the music closed, she clapped until the rest of the audience had stopped and until her hands were hot and blotched with red. She clapped until everyone was staring at the girl with lightning-coloured hair and a ladder in her stocking, whose eyes and shoes lit up the whole of the second row.

There was a something in the music that felt familiar to Sophie. 'It feels,' she said to Charles, 'like home. Do you see what I mean? Like fresh air.'

'Does it? Then I think,' said Charles, 'we must get you a cello.'

The cello they bought was small, but still too large to play comfortably in her bedroom. Charles unstuck the

skylight in the attic, and on the days on which it did not rain, Sophie climbed on to the roof and played her cello, up amongst the leaf-mould and the pigeons.

When the music went right, it drained all the itch and fret from the world and left it glowing. When she did stretch and blink and lay her bow down hours later, Sophie would feel tougher, and braver. It was, she thought, like having eaten a meal of cream and moonshine. When practice went badly, it was just a chore, like brushing her teeth. Sophie had worked out that the good and bad days divided half and half. It was worth it.

Nobody bothered her up on the rooftop. It was flat grey slate, with a stone balustrade running round the edge. The balustrade came up to Sophie's chin; people below, looking up, could see only a shock of bright hair, and a bowing elbow.

'I love the sky.' Sophie said it one night without thinking, at dinner. She bit her tongue; other girls laughed if you said things like that.

But Charles only laid a slice of pork pie on the Bible

and nodded. He said, 'I'm glad.' He added a dollop of mustard, and handed Sophie the book. 'Only weak thinkers do not love the sky.'

Almost as soon as she could walk, Sophie could climb. She started with the trees, which are the quickest route to the sky. Charles came with her. He was not a 'no-don't, hold-tighter' sort of man. He stood underneath her and shouted. 'Higher, Sophie! Yes, bravo! Watch out for the birds! Birds look wonderful from underneath!'

CHAPTER FOUR

The original cello case, Sophie's life raft, was kept at the foot of her bed. For her eleventh birthday, Charles sanded away the mildew and bought some paint.

'What colour?' he asked.

'Red. Red is the opposite of sea-colours.' It was difficult for Sophie to love the sea.

Charles painted the cello case the brightest red he could find, and set a lock on it. She stacked her precious things inside, and midnight snacks. She opened it only as a treat, or if she had one of her dark sea-nightmares.

If Sophie had known how important the cello case would prove to be, she would probably not have stored honey in it, which always manages to leak. But she did not know: it is impossible, Charles always said, to know everything.

Charles warned her not to think too much of the cello case. 'Be careful not to treasure the wrong things in life,' he said. 'We cannot tell if it is rightfully yours, Sophie. You may not be able to keep it; someone may claim it.'

'Yes, I know!' Sophie grinned. 'Someone *will* claim it. My mother will. When she comes.' Sophie spat on her palm and crossed her fingers for luck. It was like a reflex; she spat and crossed them a hundred times each night.

'The case may not have belonged to your mother. It

might have been snatched up by her as the ship went down. Women very rarely play the cello, Sophie. In fact, I have never heard of a woman who does. A violin is more usual for a woman.'

'No,' said Sophie. 'It was a cello. I know it was. I remember. I remember her fingers on the bow.'

Charles bowed his head in a courteous nod, as he always did when he disagreed. 'I remember the ship well, Sophie. I remember the band. But I do not remember, Sophie, any women with cellos.'

'But I do.'

'Sophie, no. The band was made up of men with moustaches and greased hair.'

'I *remember*, Charles! I do!'

'I know.' Charles's face was too sad to look at. Sophie scowled at her ankles instead. 'But, dear heart, you were a baby.'

'That doesn't mean I don't remember. I saw her, Charles, I really *did*. I remember the cello.' The arguments were always the same. How did you make people believe you? Sophie thought. It was too slow, and too unwieldy. It was impossible.

'I saw her floating. I did!' She balled her fists. If she had not loved him so much, she would have spat at him.

'And yet, my child, I did not see her. I was there too.' He sighed so deeply that his breath ruffled the curtains. 'I know it's hard, Sophie. Life is so hard. My God, life is the hardest thing in the world! That is a thing people should mention more often.'

Almost every night, Sophie went mother-watching. She snuffed the candle, and sat on the window sill with her legs swinging, watching the mothers on her street go by. The best ones had faces full of wit. Sometimes they carried sleeping children; fat babies, and toddlers with legs stuck out at peculiar angles. Sometimes they sang as they passed by under Sophie's dangling feet.

That evening, though, Sophie took out her sketchbook. It was leather, and soft from being kept under her pillow. She drew in it every birthday.

Sophie's pencil was bluntish, and she chewed at the lead to sharpen it. Then she closed her eyes, and tried

to remember. She drew a pair of black trousers, worn thin at the knee ('worn at the knee' is surprisingly difficult to draw, but she did her best) and on top of them the torso and head of a woman. She added hair. She had no coloured pencils, but she bit at a hangnail and used a little blood to paint it red. Then, with her pencil over the face, Sophie hesitated.

'Oh,' she whispered. And then, 'Think.' And then, 'Please.' But she could remember only a blur. At last Sophie drew a tree blowing in the wind, and then drew hair blowing across the face.

Mothers are a thing you need, like air, she thought, *and water.* Even paper mothers were better than nothing; even imaginary ones. Mothers were a place to put down your heart. They were a resting stop to recover your breath.

Under her picture, Sophie wrote 'my mother'. Her finger was still bleeding, so she drew a flower behind the woman's ear, and coloured it red.

Every night before she went to sleep, Sophie told herself stories in her head, in which her mother

returned to find her. They were long and difficult to recall in the morning, but they ended in dancing. When she remembered her mother, she always remembered dancing.

CHAPTER FIVE

By the time Sophie's twelfth birthday came around, she had almost stopped breaking plates, and the books had been moved from the kitchen back to Charles's study. Charles called her in there to give her his present. It stood on the desk, a square tower wrapped in newspaper.

'What is it?' It looked the size of a bathroom cabinet, but even from someone as unusual as Charles that seemed an unlikely gift.

'Open it.'

Sophie tore off the paper. 'Oh!' Her breath got tangled up somewhere on the way out. It was a stack of

books, each bound in a different coloured leather. The leather glowed, despite the grey day outside.

'There are twelve. One for each year.'

'They're beautiful. But … Charles, weren't they terribly expensive?' They looked as though they would be warm to touch. Leather like that wasn't cheap.

Charles shrugged. 'Twelve is the right age to start collecting beautiful things. Each of these,' he said, 'was a favourite of mine.'

'Thank you! Thank you.'

'It's the things you read at the age you are now which stick. Books crowbar the world open for you.'

'They're perfect.' Sophie turned them over. She sniffed the insides. The paper smelt of brambles and tin kettles.

'I'm glad you think so. Although, if you turn down

the corners of the pages like that I shall have to bludgeon you to death with *Robinson Crusoe*.'

When she had examined the last one (it was *Grimm's Fairy Tales*, and the illustrated plate in the front looked promising), Charles went to the window sill and came back with a carton of ice cream. It was the size of Sophie's head.

'Happy birthday, my child.' Sophie dipped in a finger; which was not allowed, but could probably be got away with on her birthday. It was rich and sweet. Sophie dug out a chunk with Charles's ruler, and grinned up at him.

'It's perfect. Thank you. It tastes exactly like birthdays should taste.'

Charles believed food was better eaten in beautiful places: in gardens, or in the middle of lakes, or on boats. 'I have a theory,' he said, 'that the best place to eat ice cream is in the rain on the outside box of a four-horse carriage.'

Sophie squinted at him. It was sometimes difficult to tell if Charles was joking. 'Is it?'

'You don't believe me?' said Charles.

'No, I don't.' Sophie struggled to keep a straight face. She could feel a laugh rising. It was like a sneeze; it filled her chest.

'Well, neither do I, to be honest. But it's possible,' said Charles. 'You and I will go out and test it. Never ignore a possible!'

'Fantastic!' Four-horse carriages were, Sophie thought, the best invention in the world. They made you feel like a warrior-queen. 'Can we ask to have the horses gallop?'

'We can. Though I suggest that you change into your trousers first. Those skirts are fascinating creations; it's as though you've mugged a librarian,' said Charles.

'Yes! I'll be quick.' Sophie gathered up her books into her arms. She could only just see over them. 'And then?'

'And then we will locate a cab. Very luckily, it happens to be raining.'

Charles, it turned out, was right. The rain lashed against them as they thundered round corners, and

made her ice cream run down over her wrist. It whipped her hair into wet snakes behind her. It made eating a challenge, but Sophie liked a challenge.

When they returned, streaming with water and stuffed with ice cream, there was a letter on the doormat. One look at the envelope made Sophie certain it was not a birthday card. All the happiness went out of her in a *whoosh*.

Charles read it with a tight-set face.

'What is it?' Sophie tried to read over his shoulder, but he was too tall. 'Who's it from? What do they want?'

'I'm not quite sure.' His face was transformed. He was unrecognisable as the man he had been only a minute before. 'It seems there is to be an inspection.'

'Of what? Of me?'

'Of us. It's from the National Childcare Agency. They say they have doubts about my ability to care for you, now that you are a young woman. They think I will be unable to teach you how to behave like a lady.'

'What? But that's crazy!'

'Governments often are.'

'I'm only just twelve! I'm practically still eleven.'

'Nonetheless, they intend to come.'

'Who is they? Who sent it?'

'Two men; one is called Martin Eliot. The other name I can't read.'

'But why? Why should two strangers get to decide about me? They don't know me! They're just men!'

'Men! I know these sorts of people. They're not men. They're moustaches with idiots attached.'

Sophie snorted with snotty laughter. She wiped her eyes. 'So what do we do?'

'I suppose we should clean.' Together, she and Charles looked around the hall. It was clean enough already, she thought, if you didn't count the poems she had copied on to the wallpaper, or the spiderwebs. Sophie liked spiders, and always dusted around them.

'Do I have to move the spiders?'

'I fear so,' said Charles. 'And I will have to cut the ivy.' Last year an ivy vine had worked its way in through the window, and spread over one wall in the hall. It had settled like a Sunday hat over the portrait of Charles's grandmother. Sophie loved it.

'Could you leave the part growing on Grandmother Pauline? They wouldn't notice, would they?'

'I can try, certainly.' But Charles was clearly not thinking of grandmothers. 'And then there's you, Sophie.'

'What about me?' Sophie felt herself flushing. 'Is there something wrong with me?'

'To me, of course, you are as close to perfect as a human can be. But I have a suspicion – though please do correct me if I'm wrong – that your hair will not meet with approval. No, not the front – here, at the back.'

Sophie groped around the back of her head. 'What's wrong with it?'

'Nothing is wrong with it, exactly. It's just that it resembles a ball of string. I believe hair is more usually described as a curtain. Or a wave.'

'Oh!' It was true, she supposed. She had never read about a heroine with balls of hair. 'Leave it to me.'

That night, Sophie went to battle with her hair. At first, her hair seemed to be winning. The knot was at the base of her neck, the most awkward place to reach.

This was usually the way with knots. Grimly, Sophie tugged, until she had a handful of hair in her lap, but still the knot was enormous. She pulled vengefully, and the comb snapped in two and stayed there, hanging in her hair. She swore, under her breath. '*Damn.*'

Sophie ran down to the kitchen, and found the scissors. She wove them into the middle of the knot, and bit down on her tongue for courage, and cut. It was surprisingly satisfying. When she had cut out the comb and most of the knot, she plaited her hair into a thick rope over her shoulder. Unless you looked closely, she thought, you would barely notice. She felt gingerly at her scalp. Being ladylike was a painful enterprise.

On the day of the inspection, Sophie scrubbed at her hands until her fingernails shone and she had rubbed half the skin off her knuckles. Charles polished her shoes with candle wax and a lump of coal, and, as they had no iron, pressed her clothes with a hot brick. Charles mopped the floor and Sophie soaped the walls until she had taken half the pattern off the wallpaper. She placed jars full of flowers all over the house. Everything smelt of rose petals and soap.

'I think it looks fine,' she said. Sophie had always loved the house, and it seemed especially handsome today. 'I think it looks perfect.'

Then they hovered by the door, unable to sit still. At the last minute, a thought occurred to Sophie.

'How long do I have until they come?' she asked Charles.

'Three minutes, or thereabouts. Why?'

'I'll be right back.' She took the stairs four at a time. In her bedroom, she powdered her nose with talcum powder, and rubbed red paint on her cheeks and lips. There was no mirror. She hoped it looked right.

Charles blinked when she came down. Sophie's suspicions that her cheeks were more 'clown' than 'gracious young lady' deepened, but before either had time to say anything the doorbell rang.

The woman on the doorstep had a clipboard, and an expression like a damp sock. The man next to her had a briefcase and elaborate facial hair. Sophie thought he looked faintly familiar.

Charles whispered, 'Moustache', and Sophie fought not to laugh.

They led the pair into the sitting room. The couple refused all offers of tea, and began their questioning at once. Sophie winced away from them. It was like being under fire.

'Why isn't the child at school?' said the woman.

Sophie waited to see if Charles would answer. When he didn't, she said, 'I don't go to school.'

'Why not?' said the man.

'I learn from Charles.'

'Do you have proper lessons?' The woman looked sceptical.

'Yes!' said Sophie. 'Of course I do.' A useful sentence popped into her head. 'Charles says, without knowledge, you see only half the world.'

'Hmph. And these lessons take place every day?'

'Yes,' lied Sophie. In fact, they did lessons whenever either of them remembered. Sophie found it very easy to forget.

'Can you read?' said the woman.

'Yes, of course!' That was stupid. Sophie couldn't remember not being able to read, any more than she could remember not being able to walk.

'Can you do mathematics?'

'Um. Yes,' said Sophie. That was true. Sort of. 'Although I hate the seven times table. I like the eights and nines, though.'

'Can you recite your catechism?'

'No.' Sophie's insides grew colder. 'I don't know what that is. Is he a poet? I can do most of Shakespeare, if you'd like.'

'No, thank you. That will not be necessary. Can you cook?'

Sophie nodded.

'Plain cooking, pastry, a fine trifle for dinner parties?'

'Um. Yes, I think so.' It wasn't a lie, she told herself firmly. She'd never made a trifle, but anyone who could read could cook, as long as you had the right books.

'You can't be eating well; you slouch, and you're too pale. Why is she so pale?'

For the first time, Charles spoke. 'She is not too pale. She is cut from the stuff of the moon.'

The woman snorted; the man was distracted,

looking around the room. 'Is this where you do lessons?' he asked Sophie.

'We mostly do them –' She had been going to say, 'on the roof', but Charles widened his eyes in warning, and his head gave the subtlest of shakes. 'Yes,' she said. 'Mostly in here.'

'Then where do you keep your blackboard?'

Sophie couldn't think of a convincing answer to that one. She told the truth. 'We don't have a blackboard.'

'And how do you expect to learn anything without a blackboard?' asked the woman.

'Well, I have books. And paper. And,' Sophie said, brightening, 'I'm also allowed to write on the walls, and draw, as long as I don't do it in the parlour. Or the hall, unless I do it behind the coat stand.'

For some reason, the woman was not appeased by this. She stood, and turned to the man. 'Shall we begin? I dread to think what we'll find.'

The pair marched through the house as though they were planning to buy it. They inspected the sheets for holes and the curtains for dust, and looked in the larder. They took notes of the rows of cheeses and jars of

jam. Finally, they marched up to Sophie's attic room, and looked through her chest of drawers.

The woman drew out the red trousers, and the man shook his head sadly. The green pair – which had accrued some interesting stains around the ankle – made the woman shudder.

'Unacceptable!' she said. 'I find it shocking, Mr Maxim, that you let this go on.'

Sophie said, 'But he doesn't *let it go on*, at all. I mean – they're mine. They're nothing to do with Charles.'

'Please hold your tongue, child.'

Sophie longed to hit her. Charles moved to stand closer to Sophie, but he said nothing. He had barely spoken; and he kept silence all the way downstairs, and only as he shook their hands did he speak a few words to the inspectors. Sophie strained, but could not hear. She closed the door behind them, and sank down on the mat.

'What did they say? Did I do all right?' She chewed on the end of her plait. 'I hated them, didn't you? I wanted to spit. That man! He had a face like a baboon.'

'He did seem excellent proof of the theory of evolution, didn't he? And the woman! I have met wrought-iron railings with more human generosity.'

'What were they saying, when they left?'

'They said they are going to submit a report.'

'That wasn't all, though, was it? You were talking for longer than that.'

'I think we'd better have a talk. Where is the best place for talking? The kitchen?'

Sophie didn't want to be anywhere the inspectors had passed through. The house felt damp and clammy in their wake. 'No, the roof.'

'Of course. I'll fetch some whisky. Why don't you run down to the kitchen, and fetch the cream jug? It helps to have cream, I think, on days like these.'

Sophie ran. The cream jug was cooling in the ice-box. There was jam, and a loaf fresh from the oven; she added that. She found Charles perched on the chimney pot.

'Sit down. Have a little whisky.' He looked about the rooftop for a glass, then handed her the bottle. 'Take a gulp.' The whisky made Sophie cough and spit, but he

said, 'Think of it as medicine. Yes, well done. Are you all right?'

'Yes, of course. What's going on? What did they say?'

'Sophie. You must try to believe what I am going to tell you. You must try to understand. Can you do that for me?'

'Of course I can,' said Sophie. She stared at him indignantly. 'Why wouldn't I?'

'Don't be too sure, my love. Believing things is a talent.'

'Fine. I'll believe you. What is it?'

'Have some bread and jam. You can dip it in the cream jug.'

'What *is* it, Charles?'

Charles took some bread and rolled it between his finger and thumb. 'First of all: it will break my heart if they take you away. You have been the great green adventure of my life. Without you my days would be unlit.' He glanced down at her. 'Do you understand that, Sophie? Do you believe me?'

Sophie nodded. She flushed, in the way she always

did when people said nice things about her. 'Yes. I think I do.'

'But there is nothing I can do to stop these people. You are not legally mine. Legally, you are the property of the state. Do you understand that?'

'No, I don't. That's stupid!'

'I could not agree more. It is nonetheless the case, my child.'

'How can I belong to the state? The state isn't a person. The state can't love anyone.'

'I know. But, I believe, they intend to take you. The pair didn't say anything definite. But they hinted.'

Sophie's whole body suddenly felt cold. 'They can't.'

'They can, my darling. Governments can do both great and stupid things.'

'What if we ran away? To another country? We could go to America.'

'They'd stop us, Sophie. They would tell the police I was kidnapping you.'

'How do you know? I bet they wouldn't!' Sophie jumped to her feet and tugged at his hand, his sleeve, his hair. 'Let's leave. We can just go, Charles. We don't

need to tell anyone. Before they send in their report. Please!' He hadn't moved. She took hold of his sleeve. '*Please.*'

'I'm so sorry, dear heart.' He looked twice as old as he had looked this morning, and she almost heard his neck bone creak as he shook his head. 'They would come and fetch you back, my darling. There are people in this world who come out in a rash at the sight of a broken rule. Miss Eliot is one such person. Martin Eliot is another.'

Sophie jumped up. '*Eliot!* I knew he looked familiar! Charles, do you think they're related?'

'Good Lord! Yes, in fact, quite possibly. My God! She once said her brother worked in government.'

'The witch!' Somehow, the idea of Miss Eliot helped. Anger was easier than misery. 'I won't give up, you know.' It made her feel tougher, and meatier, just to say it. 'I won't go.'

It was one thing to vow to be tough. When the letter came, toughness felt very difficult.

It arrived on a grey Monday morning. It was addressed to Charles, but she would have opened it anyway, had he not taken it gently from her. She watched his face, but it was wary and tight: impossible to guess.

'Can I see? Let me see?' she asked, before he could possibly be finished. 'What does it say? Is it good? Can I stay? You have to say I can. Let me see?'

Charles said, 'It's … it's not …' For once, he seemed to be without words. He handed it to her. Sophie held it up to the light.

Dear Mr Maxim,

We, the undersigned, write to inform you of changes in our policy on the guardianship of female persons aged between twelve and eighteen years.

Sophie scowled. 'Why do they have to talk like that?' She hated official letters. They made her feel nervous. The people who wrote them sounded like they had filing cabinets where their hearts should be.

'Read on, Sophie.' Charles's voice was darker than usual.

The committee has come to the unanimous conclusion that a young woman should not be raised by a single man unrelated to her, except in unusual circumstances. In the case of your ward, Sophia Maxim, it was felt certain elements of her upbringing have been absolutely unsuitable for a female child.

'What do they mean, "certain elements"?' Sophie stabbed at the paper with her finger. 'I don't understand!'

'I don't know. I can guess.'

'They mean my trousers, don't they?' she said. 'That's mad! They're evil!'

'Keep reading,' said Charles.

We must therefore inform you that your ward will be removed from your charge and enrolled in St Catherine's Orphanage in north Leicestershire. Non-compliance will result in a court order and a

maximum of fifteen years penal servitude. The committee's decision is final and effective immediately.

'Penal servitude? What does that mean?'

'Jail,' said Charles.

The Childcare Officer of your borough, Miss Susan Eliot, will collect your ward on Wednesday the fifth of June.

Yours sincerely,

Martin Eliot

Sophie felt suddenly hollow. She fished about for something to say. 'They spelled my name wrong.'

'They did.'

'If they have to break my heart, they could at least have spelled my name right.' She looked at Charles. He did not seem to be reacting.

'Charles?' A tear was making its way down her face. She licked it angrily away. She said, 'Please. Please say something.'

'So you understood the letter?'

'They're taking me away from you. They're taking you away from me.'

'They intend to try, certainly.'

She didn't want to touch the letter. She dropped it, and stood on it. Then she picked it up and read it again. She couldn't bear that 'absolutely unsuitable'. 'Do you think if I'd worn skirts? And if I didn't slouch? Or if I was prettier? Or, I don't know, sweeter? Would they have let me stay?'

Charles shook his head. She was astonished to see that he was silently weeping.

'What now?' She slipped her hand into his pocket, and drew out his handkerchief and placed it in his hand. 'Here. Charles, please say something. What do we do now?'

'I am so sorry, my child.' She had never seen a man look so white. 'I fear there is nothing.'

Quite suddenly Sophie couldn't bear it. She pelted up to her bedroom, tripping over the stairs. The tears in her eyes were making the world blur. Before she had time to think, Sophie grabbed hold of the poker and swung it at the cello case. It split with a crack. She

swung again, at the pitcher of water beside her bed, which shattered over her blanket and pillow. Sophie heard an exclamation below, and footsteps running up the stairs. She stamped and kicked. The case splintered and shards of painted wood flew across the room.

If you have never broken up a wooden box with a poker, it is worth trying. Slowly, Sophie felt her breath become more manageable.

'I won't go,' she whispered with each swing. 'I *won't*.'

After a while, although the tears and snot still ran down her face, they did not choke her. She found a rhythm – smash, breathe, crash, breathe.

'I won't *go*,' she whispered. 'No.' Smash. 'No.' Crash. '*No*.'

It took her some minutes to realise that Charles was standing in the doorway.

'Still alive, dear heart?'

'Oh! I was just –'

'Quite. Very sensible.' He surveyed the room, then led her by the hand to the bathroom. 'This calls for hot water.'

He would say nothing else, and Sophie could think

of nothing to do but to sit curled on a pile of towels, hiccupping and sniffing, while he put every pot they owned on the stove downstairs to boil, and added dried lemon peel and mint to the tub until it steamed. 'Stay in for half an hour. I have some things to attend to.'

Sophie couldn't bear to sit still in the tub. Instead she stamped to the window and back again, and thumped the wall, until Charles's voice floated up the stairs. 'Get in the tub, Sophie, and do some splashing. You will be surprised at what a difference splashing can make.'

Sophie had forgotten that the bathroom floorboards were directly above the kitchen. She sighed, and undressed, tugging vindictively at her boots. 'All right!' she called. 'I'm in now.'

Having said it, she had to get in or it would be a lie. The hot water came up to her belly button, and the lemon peel lapped against her legs. Once her body was covered in hot water, all the fight seemed to go out of it. Sophie sagged, and lay in the tub. Her heart sagged too. She could think of nothing.

When, at last, she clambered out, she made it only

as far as her bedroom rug before her legs collapsed and she dropped down, still wrapped in her towel. She lay there, half awake, and went on with her staring at nothing.

Gradually, the nothing changed into a something. A small dot of light was playing against the wall, and she had been staring at it unseeingly for many minutes.

She turned back to the pile of splintered wood that had once been her cello case to see what was casting the reflection. Then all the blood returned to her, and Sophie leaped up.

Still half-glued to the green baize lining was a long shard of painted wood. Sophie seized it, catching a splinter in her thumb. '*Ach!* Damn.'

Under the green baize, there was a brass plaque nailed to the wood. The light had been glancing off it and reflecting a pinprick of sun on the far side of the room.

On the plaque was an address. It was not in English.

Sophie had to lay the scrap of wood on the table to

read it. Her hands were shaking too much to hold it steady.

FABRICANTS
D'INSTRUMENTS À CORDES
16 RUE CHARLEMAGNE
LE MARAIS
PARIS

291054

Sophie found Charles in his study. He was sitting by the window with a newspaper in his hands, but his eyes did not seem to see it. Rain was blowing in and blurring the print on the front page, and he was doing nothing to shield himself.

Sophie ran to him, but he did not turn round. He only blinked, and his dark eyes were blank. Frightened, Sophie clambered on to the arm of his chair, tugged at his sleeve. She later thought she might even have chewed at his eyebrows in a bid to get attention.

'Look! Charles, look!'

Slowly, his eyes woke up. He smiled, just a little. 'What am I looking at?'

'This!'

Charles looked about for his glasses, then, when they did not appear, held it very close to his nose. 'Le Marais, Paris. What is this, Sophie?'

'It was French! The cello was French!'

'Where did you find this?'

'We have to go to France! Right now!' She was choking and breathless. 'Today!'

'Sit down, Sophie, and explain.'

Sophie sat: on Charles's feet, so he would not be able to move. Her mouth was dry, and she had to chew on her tongue until she had enough saliva to talk. Then, as steadily as she could, Sophie explained.

It took Charles less than a second to see her meaning. He leaped to his feet, spilling Sophie into a heap on the hearthrug.

'My God! Sweet singing salamanders, Sophie! You brilliant creature. Why didn't it occur to me that she might be French? I feel I need some whisky. Oh good Lord.'

Sophie turned a backwards roll under the desk. 'What if she's living in Paris?'

'What indeed! It's possible, Sophie. I don't say it's likely, my darling – you know that the cello case still may not be hers – but it's just possible. France, of course, my God!'

'And never ignore a possible!'

'Exactly! Oh my darling creature, what a discovery.' He looked at the letter, still lying on the desk. 'We need to get out of here, at any rate.'

'To Paris?' Sophie crossed every finger and every toe she possessed.

'Of course. Where else? Paris, Sophie! Quick! To packing! Gather up your best pants and your whitest socks!'

It was like a bugle call. Sophie sprang up. Then she said, 'I don't think I've got any that are still white.'

'Then we'll buy new ones when we get there!'

'Paris pants! Yes, please.' Sophie laughed, but the letter from Martin Eliot was lying on the table. It seemed to watch her. She said. 'Will they come after us?'

'Perhaps. Yes. Quite probably. That's why we'll leave tomorrow.'

'What, really?'

'Yes.'

'But truly?'

'I wouldn't joke about such things.' Charles spread the newspaper open at the page with notices of trade, weather, ship departures. 'And if they do choose to follow us – or, which is more likely, alert the Paris police – it won't be for at least two or three days.'

'Days?' Sophie had hoped for weeks. Surely, it would be weeks.

'Days. We need to be wary, Sophie, but we are at an advantage.' He scratched an X next to a column of boat times and high tides, and closed the paper. His eyes were glinting with such excitement that it was like warming herself at the fire. 'Organisations, Sophie, are much less clever than human beings. Especially when that human being is you. Remember that.'

CHAPTER SIX

The journey was not easy. Very few journeys are, Sophie thought, and they are made even more difficult when you are planning to skip a country illegally in broad daylight.

'Pack light,' said Charles. 'If we are seen leaving, we must look like we're going to the dentist.'

'The dentist? We never go to the dentist.'

'To a concert, then. One bag and nothing else.'

So Sophie took only her cello; she rolled up jerseys and trousers as tightly as she could, and squeezed them into the corners of the cello case. When she was

finished there was room for only one thing more; should she take her notebook, or a dress, for just in case? 'A dress is camouflage,' she told herself. 'You never know when you'll need a disguise.' Grudgingly, Sophie added it, and snapped shut the case.

Charles carried only his briefcase. Judging by the way he loaded it into the taxi cab, it was heavy. As they pulled away, Sophie thought she saw the curtain next door drop back, and a figure jerk out of sight. She gasped, and looked straight ahead. As they clattered down the street she crossed her fingers and sat on them, for luck.

The train station, when Sophie pulled her case into it, was too full of shouting people and steam. 'Oh,' said Sophie. 'Oh, no.' She said it very softly. Crowds

made her ache. They were too much like a sinking ship. 'Oh, help.' She felt a strong urge to scramble up the walls and hide behind the station clock.

Charles, though, was unworried. His eyes were very bright. He said, 'Lord, it's impressive, isn't it? Smell that smell! Engine oil, Sophie!' Then he took in Sophie's taut face and clenched elbows.

'All serene, my child?'

'Of course! Sort of. Almost.' Sophie winced as a horde of boys went roaring by, hitting each other. 'Not really.'

'Do you know, I think the best thing to do in stations is to buy a handful of your favourite food, and then find a corner to sit in and stare at the ceiling.'

'Stare at the ceiling? Why?'

'Railway stations tend to have fantastically beautiful ceilings.' Sophie tilted her head, and her hat fell off. It was true. The ceiling was a maze of glass and bright iron. It looked like a hundred pianos.

Charles felt in his pockets. From a jumble of string and paper and boiled sweets, he extracted some coins. 'Here – there's a sixpence. Or, wait – there's a shilling,

and you can buy some tea. Ask for it hot enough to burn your pipes, or it won't be drinkable.'

'Yes – thank you, of course – but *wait*, Charles! Where are you going?'

'To find a porter and secure our tickets.'

'What if I lose you?'

'Then I will find you again.'

'But what if you can't find me?' Sophie laid a hand on his overcoat. 'Charles, wait, don't go!' She hated herself when she was like this, but her nerves were chewing at her insides.

'Sophie, you have hair the colour of a lightning bolt!' He smiled. His smile, today, was a very good one. 'You are not easily missable.'

At the food stall, Sophie hesitated between an enormous Chelsea bun and those round biscuits with red-jam centres that Miss Eliot said were for common children. Sophie had never tried them, but they glinted like rubies.

The woman behind the counter was a reassuring presence. She had a red rash on her cheeks, and nice eyes.

'Chelsea bun, love? Eclair? Strawberry biscuits?'

The thought of what Miss Eliot would say restored Sophie's courage. 'Biscuits, please. Six.'

'There y'are, love. Don't eat them all at once, pet, or you'll be making a closer acquaintance with the station privy'.

Sophie nodded seriously. She bit into one, and found they glued her teeth together in a wonderful way. They did not taste remotely like strawberries, but they did taste like adventure.

'Going anywhere exciting, dear?' said the woman, clanking around in her apron for change.

Sophie tried to say, 'Paris', through her sticky mouthful. She glanced at the station clock. 'Half an hour and counting.'

'Hunting, did you say? That'll be nice.'

Sophie's teeth were now well and truly jammed shut. She only smiled gooily and nodded. It was true, in a way. She was going mother-hunting.

'God and good luck go with you, then,' said the woman. She wrapped a Chelsea bun in newspaper and

slipped it across to Sophie. 'For luck. Most luck happens on a full stomach.'

The train was twice the size Sophie had expected, and green. It was the green that emeralds and dragons usually come in; which felt to Sophie like a good omen.

'Look for carriage six, Sophie,' said Charles. 'You are Compartment A. I am told it is usually reserved for the children of the Duke of Kent, but this summer they are shooting things in Scotland. You have it to yourself.'

They edged past porters with straight backs and starched collars, towards the front and the engine. There was a narrow corridor running the whole length of the train, with sliding doors leading to the compartments. Sophie tried not to get in the way; and tried not to look too excited; and tried not to look too much like an illegal runaway. None of the three was easy.

'Here!' Charles manoeuvred her cello case through the door, and turned. His whole face was sparking. 'It was the only one left, Sophie. I hope you don't dislike it.'

Sophie peered round his shoulder. Then she stared. 'Dislike it? It's like an imaginary game!' People were pressing past in the corridor outside; Sophie ignored them. 'It's so ... *gilt*. It's a palace!'

Charles laughed, and pulled her inside, and shut the door on the rest of the train. 'A very small palace. The travel-sized version, perhaps.'

The carriage was beautiful. Everything was child-sized, and made with the delicacy and detail of witch-craft. Sophie tried to look as if she was used to such things – at least while the porter was watching them – but it was impossible, for it was the most polished-clean, gold-edged thing she had ever seen. The pillows were round and fat as a goose's stomach. The mirror was edged in gold; in fact there was almost as much gold edge as mirror. Sophie tapped it. It sounded solid.

'And see your chamber pot,' said Charles. 'It's worth a look.'

She squatted to look under the bed. There, buck-led securely to the wall, was a golden chamber pot with red carnations painted round the rim.

'See?' said Charles. 'Even your night-time peeing is accessorised.'

'But where do you sleep? Here, also?' The carriage had two bunks, but they were child-sized. Most of Charles would dangle off the end.

'I will share a bunk with an undertaker from Luxembourg. A lugubrious sort of fate, but I won't die of it; and after all, it could have been worse. He could have been Belgian.' Charles smiled down at her. 'They were the only beds available for three weeks. I thought it would be better than the itch of waiting.'

'Yes!' Waiting would have been impossible, she thought. She would have died. 'Yes, thank you!'

'Now, all serene?' asked Charles. Having no handkerchief, he fished out a clean sock and blew his nose on it. It sounded, to Sophie, like the trumpet of hope. 'You have everything you need?'

'Yes, I think so. Although, actually' – her stomach rumbled – 'have we got anything to eat?'

'Of course! How could I forget? The best part of any journey is the food. There's a restaurant car, but it

won't open for a few hours. I smuggled in as much as I could.' Charles crossed to the wooden desk set into the wall and began to empty his pockets. First, six apples; then sausage rolls, shedding their pastry all over his coat, and a thick slab of yellow cheese. From the back of his fob watch Charles extracted a screw of salt. Finally, like a conjuror, he took from under his hat half a roast chicken, wrapped in oiled paper.

'Oh, heaven! Oh, wonderful!' Sophie added her biscuits to the pile; but kept back her Chelsea bun for later. She arranged the rest into a tower. 'There!' It reached up to her nose. 'This is perfect.'

'Now, have we got everything?'

'Um.' Sophie had just taken a mouthful of cheese. The taste was fantastic; salty and creamy, both, together. The train shuddered, and began to steam forwards. She had Charles, and roast chicken, and an adventure. Sophie spoke around her mouthful. 'Everything,' she said.

At Dover, they changed from the train to a boat. The weather was choppy. The sea rumbled in front of them.

It was grey, and smelt wild. Sophie tried not to look down at it. She tried not to think of dead women.

'All serene?' said Charles.

Sophie nodded, but she couldn't speak.

To make things worse, amongst the passengers on the boat was a policeman. It was impossible, she told herself, that he had come for her; he was probably on holiday; but he still made her shiver. To be out of his sight, Sophie inched away down the boat until she was alone on the outside deck. She tried to ignore the sea. Ignoring the sea, though, is like ignoring a man with a gun: it cannot be done. It stretched out as far as the horizon, and though she squinted, Sophie couldn't see France. She gripped the rail, and tried not to panic.

Charles saw her face from halfway down the ship. His footsteps made no sound, and the hand he laid on hers was gentle as a mother's.

'Listen!' he said. 'Can you hear that?'

Sophie could only hear the sea. 'What?' Fear made her more snappish than she had wanted to be. 'What am I listening for, anyway?'

'A murmuration!' said Charles. 'A good omen.'

'A what-eration?'

'A murmuration. When the sea and wind murmur in time with one other; like people laughing in private. There, again! Did you hear that?'

Sophie was not convinced. 'Only people murmur. Sea roars. Wind blows.'

'No. Sometimes the sea and the wind murmur. The two are old friends.'

'Oh.' Sophie unpeeled her hand from the rail, and gripped Charles's. She breathed in his overcoat smell, and straightened her spine.

'When they sound together,' he said, 'it means luck. A murmuration. A good omen.'

CHAPTER SEVEN

The obvious problem did not occur to Sophie until she was standing next to Charles in the Gare du Nord with her cello case clutched to her chest.

The English porter from the train was watching the sky. 'It's due to storm again soon, Sir. I hope you brought umbrellas.'

Charles said, 'I am an Englishman. I always have an umbrella. I would no more go out without my umbrella than I would leave the house without my small intestine.'

'Then I'd get yourself to your hotel before the hour's up, Sir. I don't like the look of the sky.'

It was then that the problem occurred to Sophie. It startled her that she had not thought of it before, but she had not, in the rush, imagined further than the English border control. 'Charles,' she said, 'where are we going to sleep?'

'Very good –'

'And,' she interrupted, 'and also – what are we going to do next?'

'Very good questions, both,' Charles said. 'The first is easy. The undertaker was very helpful. He recommended a very good little hotel, near the river Seine.' He hefted his briefcase. 'We'll take a taxi cab.'

There was a row of carriages waiting by the train station. They varied in smartness; some had interesting bits of carriage-gut hanging down underneath, and others gleamed and smelt of carbolic soap. There

was one painted grey and silver that Sophie liked immediately. The horse matched the carriage, and its face was thinner and wittier than the others. It looked like Charles: though Sophie decided not to say so.

'Can we take this one?' Sophie held out her last sliver of chocolate to the grey mare. 'The horse looks like he's bored.'

'Of course.' Charles handed the driver some coins, and the man began to load the carriage with their sparse luggage. 'I must say, French horses are very good-looking,' said Charles. 'Paris is making me feel that I should brush my hair.'

Sophie looked about, at the tall trees towering over the buildings, and the cobbled streets curling off in every direction. The women's skirts hung differently to those in London; the women seemed to glide, somehow, as though they were underwater. 'Yes!' she said. 'I know what you mean. Even the pigeons are more chic than in London.' She found her insides were shivering in that way they did before Christmas. She

said, 'And when we've got to the hotel? Then what do we do?'

'Then we are going to find a bakery, Sophie, and we're going to make a plan.'

'Why a bakery? I was thinking, more like, a police station? Or, a post office, or a mayor's hall?'

'The most important part of planning is having something to eat. There would be fewer wars if prime ministers ate doughnuts at government meetings.'

'And then?' she said. 'And then what?'

'And then,' said Charles, 'we go hunting.'

High up above the Seine, thirty feet up in the air, a pair of brown eyes was watching the street below. They watched a buggy pull up to the Hotel Bost, and a girl clamber out. The eyes noted the twitch in the girl's fingers, the tense excitement in her shoulder blades. They saw her biting her teeth together in determination and dragging a cello case off the cart; and watched her jump back, flustered, out of the path of a motor car. The eyes saw her anxiously open the case, and pull out

the instrument and check it front and back; and then squat on the pavement and pluck out a thrumming tune with her finger and thumb.

The sound was soft, and almost drowned by the traffic below, but the brown eyes flickered, as though impressed.

CHAPTER EIGHT

The plan Sophie and Charles made was, of necessity, simple. Sophie wrote it out on a scrap of paper.

1. Find rue Charlemagne.

2.

Sophie's pen hesitated over '2'. Then she drew a large question mark. She underlined it in red ink, and put the list in her pocket, and went to find Charles.

Charles's room was nice, though you could not call it smart. There were two spindly chairs, on which a succession of bottoms had left their mark, and two

rugs, on which a good deal of expense had been spared. Even the bedside candles looked second-hand, but the linen smelt of lavender. The wind was blowing from the river, and the air was brackish. Sophie had never felt so much at home in a hotel. Usually they gave her the shivers.

The hotel itself was a tall, gangly building, sandwiched between two more imposing blocks of apartments. It was cheap, because, as Sophie had just discovered, there was no indoor toilet, only a wooden box in the garden, but apart from that it was perfect. From the window, thin streets and pavement cafes wove away from them down towards the river.

Sophie sat on Charles's bed and bounced. Above the bed there was a painting of a man in a beard that curled at the point.

'I like his beard,' she said. 'He could use it as a paintbrush.'

Charles looked up, startled. 'What?' Then he laughed. 'Did you find the bathroom?'

'Yes. We're sharing it with a family of spiders, though. And there's a bird's nest in the ceiling joist. I quite like it.'

'Good. Shall we go and explore your room? Let me carry your case. No? As you wish.'

Sophie's bedroom was in the attic of the hotel. There wasn't much to explore. The doorway was so small that Charles stayed outside, and let her go in alone. Once she had set down her cello case, there was barely room to stand.

'Look!' she said.

The walls were covered in ink sketches, arranged higgledy-piggledy to pick up the most possible light. They were done in quick black strokes; they looked like they were fidgeting in their frames. 'I like these. They look French.'

'They look like music,' said Charles. He tucked his

head into his neck and peered further in. Then, 'No window?'

'Skylight,' said Sophie.

A tiny four-poster bed was hung with white cotton at the sides, and open at the top. There was a window set into the slanting roof. Looking up, Sophie realised that the reason Charles hadn't seen it immediately was that it was so thickly encrusted with bird droppings on the outside that it matched the white ceiling.

'Do you think it opens?' she said.

'I can think of only one way to find out.' Charles edged his way into the room, and laid his newspaper on the bed. He set his feet on the newspaper, and prised open the catch. The window did not open when he pushed, nor when he jabbed at the hinge with his umbrella.

'Rusted hinge,' he said. 'Easily solved. It's not painted shut, so it shouldn't be a problem.'

'Do you think the hotel will have some oil?'

'It's unlikely. But we'll find you some oil tomorrow.'

'Thank you.' She stood on the bed and squinted

through the gaps in the pigeon mess. She could see red chimney pots, and blue sky. 'My heart feels too large for my body,' she said. 'It all feels so familiar, Charles, and I don't know why. It does, though. Do you believe me?'

'Paris?'

'Yes, sort of. Maybe. But I was actually thinking, the chimney pots. They look familiar; and they're such a good colour.'

Charles was a scholar, and scholars, he always said, are made to notice things. He must have heard in her voice how much she wanted to be alone, because he strode swiftly to the door. 'I'll leave you to explore. Half an hour, Sophie; and then we'll find a map, and get ourselves to rue Charlemagne. If it's near the river it can't be far from here.'

CHAPTER NINE

Rue Charlemagne was easy to find. It was ten minutes' walk; ten minutes through cobbled streets, and window boxes full of red carnations, and children eating hot buns in the road; ten minutes in which Sophie's heart looped the loop and danced a jitterbug and generally behaved in a way entirely out of her control. '*Hold steady,*' she whispered to herself. And then, 'Stop it. That's enough.'

'Did you say something?' said Charles.

'No. I was singing to the pigeons.'

The shop had a plaque above the window. There

was a violin in it, resting on a bed of silky stuff, and some flowers. Everything except the violin was covered in dust.

Inside it was the sort of over-full shop where everything looks ready to fall off the shelves. Sophie pulled in her stomach as they went in, and glanced nervously at Charles. He was so *long*: he did not always take care where he was putting his legs.

'Hello?' said Sophie, and Charles added, 'Good afternoon?'

Nobody answered. They stood stock-still, waiting. Sophie counted five minutes tick past. Every ten seconds, she called, 'Hello? Bonjour? *Hello?*'

'I think it's empty,' said Charles. 'Shall we come back later?'

'No! We'll wait.'

'Hello?' called Charles again. 'I have a cello-child here. She needs your help.'

There was a noise like a horse sneezing, and a man appeared from a door behind the counter, rubbing his eyes. He was stooped, and his paunch sat over his belt like a mixing bowl stuffed up his shirt.

'Je m'excuse!' he said. He spoke some quick sentences in French.

Sophie smiled politely but blankly. She said, 'Um.'

'Pas du tout,' said Charles.

'What did he say?' Sophie whispered.

'Ah!' the man smiled. 'I said, I was having my nap. You are English.' His accent was thickly French, but he spoke easily. 'Can I *aide* you?'

'Yes, please! At least, I hope so.' Sophie laid the plaque on the desk. She crossed all eight of her fingers. 'It's this.'

'It was screwed to the lid of a cello case,' said Charles. 'Can you tell us anything about it?'

The man did not seem at all surprised. *'Bien sûr.*

Of course.' He fingered the plaque. 'This is mine. I engraved it myself. These are tacked to the inside of the cases. Under the green baize.'

'Yes!' Sophie uncrossed her fingers, recrossed them. 'Yes, that's where it was!'

'It must be old, then,' said the man, 'because we stopped using brass ten years ago. We found it was rusting under the baize.'

'Why are they *under* the baize?' asked Charles. 'Surely that rather defeats the point?'

'But, of course: so they don't scratch the cello, but the address is there, if it is needed.'

'And' – Sophie held her breath: and then had to let it out so she could speak – 'do you remember which cello it went with? Do you remember who bought it?'

'Of course. Cellos are expensive, my child. A man will make only twenty in his whole life, perhaps. You see the serial number – 291054 – that means it was a twenty-nine inch. I have made only three such cellos in the last thirty years. The norm, as I am sure you know, is the thirty-two inch.'

'Who bought *this* one, though?' Sophie inched the plaque closer to him on the desk. 'This is the only one I care about.'

'That particular cello, I think, was bought by a woman.'

'A woman?' Sophie's insides spun about. But she held steady. 'What kind of woman?'

'A handsome kind of woman, I think.'

Charles said, 'Could you be more specific? How long ago was this?'

'About … fifteen years. Perhaps more, perhaps less. She seemed fairly normal, as beautiful women go. Beautiful women are usually a little odd, I find.'

'What else was she like?' Sophie said, 'Please? What else?'

'She was tall, I think.'

'And what else? What else?' said Sophie. She pulled the neck of her jersey up to her mouth and bit down on it.

'What else? I'm afraid nothing very much.'

'Please?' There was a roaring in Sophie's ears. 'It's important. It's *so* important!'

'Well, I remember she had a musician's fingers. Very pale, like the roots of a tree.'

'Yes? And what else?' said Sophie.

'She had short hair, and a lot of movement around the eyes.'

'What colour hair? What colour eyes?'

'Lightish, I suppose. Yellow hair. Or orange. *Je ne sais pas*.'

'Please! Please, try! It's important.'

'I would like very much to help you,' he said, 'but I must admit that I am not good at faces. I am better at instruments.' He squinted at the two of them, standing side by side in the gloom. 'But she looked, I think, very like you. Not you, Sir. *You*.'

'Are you sure?' asked Sophie. 'Do you swear you're not making it up? Swear that you're sure?'

'*Ma petite belle*: when you are old, you are rarely sure. Being sure is a bad habit.' The man smiled. His skin creaked. 'Don't go.' He lowered himself into a seat. 'I have an assistant. He was there when we sold it. He will have a better memory. These days I only remember music.'

The assistant was hard and angular where the owner was soft and wispy. The two spoke in French; then the younger man turned to Charles.

'Yes,' he said, 'I remember. Her name was Vivienne.'

A name, coming so suddenly, was like being punched. Sophie's breath left her body. She could only stare.

Charles said, 'Vivienne what?'

The man shrugged. 'I don't remember. A colour, I think. Rouge, perhaps. I don't know. Vert, perhaps. *Oui*, I think Vert.'

'Vivienne!' Sophie's insides pirouetted. *Vivienne*. It was a word to conjure with.

Charles said, 'Thank you. Do you remember anything else? Was she married? Did she have a child?'

'She was not, and she did not.' The assistant had tough eyes, and a sneering mouth. 'But she was poor – her clothes were a disgrace – and I would not be surprised to hear of any number of children. She looked the sort of person to end in trouble with the law.'

'What?' said Sophie.

He sniffed. 'She had a lawless-looking mouth.'

Charles saw Sophie's face. He intervened. 'And was she a professional musician?' he said.

The assistant shrugged. 'Women are not professional musicians in France, Sir, thank God. But she played that cello, in the shop, until I stopped her.'

Sophie said, 'You *stopped* her?'

'Little girl! Please do not take that tone with me. She was disturbing the other customers.'

'Was she good?' This man didn't seem to understand how important it was, and she wasn't sure how to make him see. She drummed on the desk with her fists. 'Was she wonderful?'

He shrugged again. 'She was a woman. Women's talents are limited.' Sophie wanted to hit him, hard, with all the muscle she had. She wanted to bludgeon him with one of the violins on the wall. The man said, 'She was peculiar.'

There was a cough. The old owner had come round from behind the desk and was standing at his assistant's elbow. He held a cello bow like a horse whip. 'Try a little harder, please, Mr Lille.'

Mr Lille flushed. 'I meant, she was peculiar in

musical terms. She played funereal marches in double time. She played Fauré's *Requiem* without the necessary dignity.'

'She did?' said Sophie.

'She did!' The owner smiled. 'I remember that! *That* I do remember! She said, she knew nothing but the funeral marches, from living near a church.'

'A church?' asked Sophie. 'Did she say which?'

'*Non*. But she said, people should be able to dance to music; so she learned the church tunes and played them double time.'

Sophie loved the sound of that. It was something she would like to do herself. 'And she was good, wasn't she? I just know she was good.' Her fingers tingled.

'Good has nothing to do with it. It was indecent,' said the assistant. 'She made solemn music frivolous. It wasn't ... *comme il faut*.'

'Could you demonstrate it for us?' said Charles.

'No,' he said, 'I could not.'

The owner straightened his back. It cracked like a revolver shot, and Sophie winced. 'I could,' he said.

Mr Lille looked staggered. 'Monsieur! Think of what your doctor said.'

'As a favour to the little girl.' He pulled a cello from its case. 'Listen.'

The music started slowly. Sophie shivered. She had never liked the *Requiem*. The old man bit his tongue, and quickened his pace. The music sped up, to a march and then to a run, until it sounded rollicking and sad at once. Sophie wanted to clap in time, but the rhythm was hard to capture. It was music that kicked and spun. 'It's like a rainstorm,' she whispered to Charles. 'That's the music a rainstorm would play.'

'Yes,' said Charles, and the man overheard and called over his playing. 'Yes, exactly, *chérie*! That is it exactly!'

Soon – far too soon for Sophie – the man put down his bow. 'There,' he said. 'Something like that. She was faster than me, I think.'

'But,' the assistant said, 'she did not play as elegantly as Monsieur Esteoule. She rushed with her bow. The young are foolish, and prize speed.'

Charles raised an eyebrow. Eyebrows can be powerful, and Mr Lille looked quelled. 'I admit,' said Mr

Lille, 'that I have never heard anyone play as quickly as the girl.'

'Vivienne,' said Sophie. She said it in a whisper. 'She was called Vivienne.'

'Yes, Vivienne,' said Monsieur Esteoule. 'I remember clearly now, I think. She was extraordinary. *Mon Dieu*, the speed! I would not have thought it possible.'

'But it was not a proper way to play,' said the assistant. 'I was *not* impressed.'

'I was,' said Monsieur Esteoule. 'I was. And I am not easily impressed.'

Sophie left Charles to do the thanking and the farewells. She couldn't speak. She needed to keep the music in her head. Sophie had a corner of her brain – it felt near the front, and to the left – in which she kept music; now she stored it away there.

CHAPTER TEN

Having a name changed everything. Charles made an appointment with the police record office for the next day. He filled in the form with neat capitals.

'*Nom du disparu*,' he said, 'That's "name of missing person": Vivienne Vert.' Then he hesitated. 'It says, "name of supplicant".'

'Is that us? What shall we put?' asked Sophie. 'Are we going to lie? We're not going to give our real names, are we?'

'Certainly not. But even then, it's rather difficult,' he said. 'Technically, my darling, we're on the run. In fact, I think perhaps you had better stay at the hotel.'

'But couldn't we just give fake names?'

'Yes, of course. But London may have sent out a wire by now, to the nearby ports. There will be descriptions.'

'But you said it would be days.'

'I said I *hoped* it would. I would still be far happier if you stayed at home.'

'Why me and not you, though?'

'I am nondescript, my darling. You are memorable. I fear you are, if you'll forgive me, spectacularly describable. The hair, you know.'

Sophie considered. She thought of waiting in her attic bedroom while Charles was gone. It made her feel sick. 'No. I have to come.'

'Are you sure?'

'I won't talk. But I have to come.'

Charles hesitated. 'Do you have a skirt?'

'Yes. At least, I have a dress.'

'Do you have a hat? Something to hide your hair?'

'Yes. Miss Eliot gave it to me. It makes me look like a poodle, though.'

'Excellent. A police description will make no mention of a poodle. Wear it.'

Sophie woke early on the next morning. She got dressed quickly; or rather, she tried to. It wasn't easy to breathe that morning. It seemed there was too much hope in her chest for the air to fit alongside.

The police headquarters was a large building. Too large, Sophie thought, and too cold. But the receptionist was sweet-faced, and Charles offered her his box of mints while they waited. She looked surprised, and then grinned and took three. Sophie refused them; it was hard enough to swallow as it was. Charles and the girl were laughing over something in French, and the sound echoed too loudly around the marble hall. Sophie wished they wouldn't. People were staring.

She moved a little further off, and pretended to read the French notices on the walls.

The receptionist was watching her. The girl tugged at Charles's lapel, and, when he politely inclined his head, she whispered in his ear. Then she looked at Sophie, and laughed again. Sophie scowled, embarrassed. The clerk appeared just as the echo of the laugh was dying, and the girl ducked her head and began straightening some papers.

'Come quickly, please,' he said. He spoke English with no trace of accent. 'I can only spare ten minutes. And you, Brigitte, should not be laughing in office hours.'

The clerk had a trick of moistening his teeth before he spoke. Like a toad, Sophie thought, eating flies. Sophie tried not to look too nervous. Her upper lip was sweating. She dodged behind Charles, and licked the sweat off.

The floor was laid in marble, and rang with the *clack* of Sophie's boots as they followed the clerk down the corridor. She tried to walk on tiptoe, but it slowed her

down by half a corridor's length. The clerk turned round and sighed, damply.

Sophie blushed. 'I'm sorry! I'm not doing it on purpose! It's just … my shoes are new.'

Charles turned round too, and walked back, and took her hand. 'Don't apologise. Your shoes are excellent; you sound like a tap dancer.'

The clerk turned away. Sophie pulled Charles down so she could whisper. 'What was the secretary saying?'

'Amongst other things, that she thought you very beautiful. I told her a little about you. She said you have the face of a warrior.'

'Oh! Then why was she laughing?'

'She wasn't laughing at you. Anyway, this place could do with a little laughing, couldn't it?'

'Yes! It's like a prison.' She gripped him tightly. 'It's like they've forgotten everything important, isn't it? I mean, forgotten that things like cats and dancing exist.'

'I know. Exactly. Let's rattle the corridors, shall we? Shall we stomp?'

'Yes!' Sophie said, and *Brave*, she told herself. *You have the face of a warrior.*

She straightened her spine, and stomped down the hall. Charles attempted a gangly two-step. He looked like a horse trying to climb a ladder. It made Sophie feel immediately better, and she jumped high, and clacked her ankles together. Charles applauded with his free hand against his thigh. The clerk sighed, pointedly, and his fringe rippled upwards, like seaweed. Sophie put out her tongue behind his back.

The clerk halted outside a room with a large brown desk in it.

'This is our interview room,' he said. 'It's newly refurbished, Sir, so please don't let your little girl touch anything.' The pictures on the walls were of men in clothes that looked too tight. One, from his face, appeared to be farting.

'It's very … clean,' said Sophie. She pulled her hat more securely over her hair. It was as though, she thought, they had deliberately painted everything grim-coloured. Even the chandelier looked depressed.

'If you'll step inside, Mr Smith,' said the clerk. 'And the little girl –' the clerk gestured to some chairs lined up in the corridor, 'the little girl will wait outside.'

'What?' said Sophie. 'No! Charles, please? *Please.*'

'Thank you, Sir,' Charles's face was blank and careful, 'but the "little girl" will join us, if she wants to.'

'I do want to stay,' said Sophie. And then, because she had remembered she wasn't supposed to talk, she glared at the clerk with her lips bitten shut.

'Please be seated, then.' The clerk was short, and his nose came up to Charles's collarbone. When he sighed this time it was hard enough to ruffle Charles's tie. 'This will not take long.'

Sophie glanced at Charles. 'Why not?' she whispered. 'That's not good, is it?'

Charles gave a tiny shake of his head. His lips formed the words, 'Be quiet, dear heart.' Sophie fell still again.

The clerk said, 'I'm afraid I must tell you, before we begin, that this is not the sort of request we welcome.'

'Oh?' said Charles. Sophie kept her eyes on him. His face was blank as a brick wall. 'Surely dealing with these requests is your job?'

'It is one small part of my job, yes,' said the clerk, 'but a request for a missing person, if you have not met

or even *seen* the missing person in question, seems absurd.'

'Does it?' said Charles. 'How fascinating.'

'You will excuse me if I say that such enquiries lead only to time-wasting and disappointment, nine times out of ten.'

'I see,' said Charles. 'And the tenth?'

'Actually I should have said, nine hundred and ninety-nine times in a thousand.'

'Quite. And the thousandth?'

'Sir, you will not be the exception. I cannot believe that such a woman exists.'

'There are thousands and thousands of things we have not believed which have turned out to be true,' said Charles. 'One should not ignore the smallest glimmer of possibility.'

'Sir. This is *im*possible. You have asked us about a woman for whom you have no birthplace, no date of birth, and no profession.'

Sophie said, 'She was a musician. You told him that, didn't you, Charles?'

'You will forgive me, Miss Smith, but women are not

musicians. We do, in fact, have records of a woman called Vivienne Vert, but –'

'You do?' Sophie sat up straight as an arrow. 'Where is she?' The clerk ignored her. 'What do they say?'

Charles repeated Sophie's question. 'What do these records say?'

'It cannot be the same woman, if what you say is true. She was not a musician. She seemed to be in minor trouble with the law.'

'What kind of trouble?' said Sophie.

'Oh, trespassing, loitering, associating with tramps and vagabonds. Anyway, she vanished thirteen years ago; suddenly no doctor's notes, no bank records. Women of her type often disappear. We have no record of a child. And we certainly have no record of this woman on board the *Queen Mary*.'

'Presumably we may see the records of the *Queen Mary*?' said Charles.

It was a simple question, but the man's face froze. The corner of his mouth twisted downwards. 'Have you any reason to, Sir?'

'Of course we do!' cried Sophie, 'I was –' She stopped.

'Yes?'

Sophie said, 'Nothing.' She was Miss Smith, of course, who had nothing to do with Sophie Maxim. 'Sorry,' she muttered. 'No.'

The clerk went back to ignoring her. Charles said, 'Curiosity is a good reason for most things, I think. Have you any reason *not* to show them?'

'Yes,' he said. Sophie watched his eyes flick to the filing cabinets and back again. 'Or, not precisely; that is to say, I believe the records may have gone down with the ship. That sort of search is not my responsibility.' His voice grew shrill. 'Paperwork, Sir, is a complicated business! I'm afraid I can't help you. No.'

'In that case, could you refer our request –'

'Coffee!' cried the man suddenly. He rang a bell. 'May I offer you some coffee before you go?'

'Thank you,' said Charles, 'but no. I would rather discuss –'

'I must insist!' His eyes were panicked. 'French

coffee is the best in the world.' The receptionist wheeled a silver trolley into the room. She winked at Sophie. 'Just put it down and go, Brigitte,' said the clerk. 'Now. What were we saying?'

Sophie took a mouthful, and tried to swallow, but found her throat had stopped working. She spat it, very quietly, back into the cup. A little of it spattered on to her white top and the clerk recoiled.

'Sorry,' she muttered. 'Too hot.'

The clerk turned his back on her, as best he could while sitting down. It looked painful. 'Now, what were we saying, Sir?' he repeated.

'*You* were saying,' said Charles, 'that you are unable to help us find the records of the *Queen Mary.* I am asking you to refer our request to someone who will feel differently.'

Pouring out the coffee had given the man time to gather his thoughts. He moistened his frog-lips. 'I cannot do that, I am afraid. That is absolutely impossible. Protocol.'

Charles nodded. 'I see,' he said. His politeness was

deadly. 'Sophie,' he said, 'could you step outside for a moment?'

'Oh! Why? Because I spat? Please, don't –'

'No,' he said gently, 'not because you spat. But please do go.'

Sophie saw his face; without a word, she stood up.

'I'll be just outside the door,' she said, and shut it behind her.

Outside, Sophie dropped to the floor, and gripped her ankles. The corridor felt colder than it had before. It felt darker. Sophie clenched her fists, and stared at the ceiling. She whispered into her knees. 'Please. *Please*. I need her.' Her heart was thumping painfully. 'That's all I want. Just her.'

There were voices coming from inside the room. Sophie shook herself, and then laid her ear against the keyhole. The metal was cold, and made her face squirm, but the keyhole was large and she could hear clearly.

The clerk was speaking. '… ridiculous. A child's imagination – a little girl –'

Then Charles's voice. 'You underestimate children. You underestimate girls. Sir, I need an appointment with the chief commissioner.'

'And you, Sir, *over*estimate your own importance. I cannot let you see the chief commissioner.'

'I see.' There was a pause. Sophie held her breath. 'The girl at reception is very charming, isn't she? She was very helpful.'

'I fail to see what that has to do with anything.'

'She mentioned your innovative brand of accounting. Your grasp of numbers really is ... unique. And your own bank account seems to appear more often than is traditional.'

There was a sputtering noise. Sophie guessed the clerk's coffee had made a reappearance.

Charles's voice said, 'I have no wish to deal in dirty things; but I feel an appointment with the chief commissioner is in both my interest and yours.'

'This is blackmail.'

'Quite,' said Charles.

'Blackmail is a felony.'

Charles said, 'Exactly.'

The clerk's voice sounded stiff and cold as a corpse. 'Is the girl worth it? Worth committing a felony?'

'She is,' said Charles evenly. 'She is bright enough to start a forest fire.'

'She seemed fairly ordinary,' said the clerk. Crouched outside, Sophie bristled.

'People usually do, until you know them,' said Charles. 'Sophie is uniquely endowed with intelligence, grit; and, at this particular moment, coffee stains. In fact, speaking of which –' A chair scraped, and Sophie just had time to stumble backwards two steps before door opened.

'Come back in, Sophie. This gentleman has good news.'

The clerk was whiter than before. His nostrils were curling. 'I can make an appointment,' he said, 'with the chief commissioner. He may be able to help you.'

'Thank you,' said Charles. 'How kind of you. Tomorrow?'

'Tomorrow is impossible. In fact, this week is very busy – I'm not sure if he –'

Charles stood. At his full height, he loomed over the

clerk. His eyebrows were at their most alarming. 'The day after tomorrow, then. Thank you. We'll be here at midday. Come, Sophie.'

For the second time that day, Sophie pulled him down to whisper. 'I haven't finished my coffee. Do I have to?'

'No,' said Charles, 'I think I'll leave mine, too. It tastes like liquidated carpet.'

'Good,' said Sophie. 'I thought it tasted like burned hair, actually.' She spat, for a second time, into the cup.

CHAPTER ELEVEN

The nights were quieter in Paris than they were in London. Sophie couldn't sleep. Once she was in bed the moonlight shone in brightly enough to read by, but Sophie stared at her book without seeing the words.

She was frightened. She told herself there was no reason to be afraid, but her pulse quickened and quickened until she couldn't breathe. Sophie tried to think of Charles, who was so kind and so amply belegged; and then she tried to think of her mother, who was perhaps only a few streets away. Neither helped. She could think only of being caught, and the horror there

would be, and the happy twist there would be on Miss Eliot's face.

Sophie heard the rest of the hotel settle into silence. She tossed in bed until her sheets and blankets were in a pile on the floor, but still she couldn't sleep.

At last, Sophie climbed on to the bed and looked closer at the skylight. They had forgotten to buy oil, and when she tugged at the window-fastening nothing happened. The hinge was rusted and flaking.

An idea came to her. Sophie whispered, 'Yes!'

She ran down the stairs two at a time. Outside the dining room she waited, listening at the door. It sounded empty; she darted in, seized the bottle of olive oil from the nearest table and was out again before a mouse in the corner had time to do more than blink.

Back in her bedroom, Sophie poured the oil over a

handful of newspaper and dabbed at the hinge. After a few minutes, nothing had happened to the hinge, but the paper disintegrated stickily in her hands. She needed something tougher.

'Cloth. I need cloth,' Sophie whispered. Perhaps the pillowcase would do? But the hotel might have strong opinions about that. Then she had a flash of inspiration: she pulled off one of her wool stockings, put it on like a glove, and tipped half the bottle of oil over it.

With her tongue sticking out between her teeth, Sophie scrubbed at the hinge. Flakes of rust began to peel off, and beneath them was bright brass. Her heart, inexplicably, began to pound. Once she had got it smooth enough, Sophie clicked back the latch – it was stiff, but the oil on her fingers helped – and pushed, hard, at the window. Nothing happened. She pushed harder. It creaked angrily, and stayed shut.

Sophie swore. She sank down to the floor. There was no reason to be so upset, she told herself. It was just a window. It probably wasn't designed to open. For no reason at all, she found herself fighting that prickling feeling behind the nose that comes before tears.

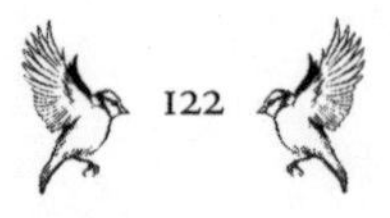

'Calm down. You're being stupid,' she told herself. 'Think.' She got to her feet, and as she did so, knocked something off her bedside table. It was the station woman's Chelsea bun. 'Oh!' whispered Sophie.

The bun was stale around the edges, but still sweet and sticky in the centre. She finished it in less than a minute.

Sophie licked her fingers (and instantly regretted it: the sugar and oil together tasted disgusting) and pulled herself to her feet. She spat on her hands, and pushed at the corners of the window frame with all her weight. She heaved. Then she leaped back as the skylight opened suddenly with a shriek.

'Yes!' she said. Without waiting to think Sophie scrambled up. She laid one knee against the ledge and one foot on the bedstead; and then she gave a one-footed jump, and both her hands scrabbled for a hold on the roof outside. Then, with a grunt of pain and a tumble, she was on to the rooftop.

Sophie crouched on hands and knees, waiting for her breath to slow. She was bleeding quite vigorously from one knee, and while she waited to stop

shaking she licked it, and tied it up with her other stocking.

The roof stretched away, flat and grey and smooth, and decorated here and there with bird droppings. There was a chimney stack, and a weathervane, and black soot layering everything. She thought the rooftop must be one of the highest for miles. A single pigeon watched her. She made a face at it. It looked haughtily at her, and turned its back.

Sophie crawled to the edge and looked out, across the city. Paris lay below her, coloured in shades of night-blue. The city was a cross-hatching of roads and squares. In the moonlight she could see the tops of bright shop awnings – they were surprisingly dirty, seen from above – and the concentric circles of two smart gentlemen's hats as they passed. *Top hats look much less stupid*, she thought, *seen from a rooftop.* And from up here, she thought, the streets looked like rivers. The river itself was quicksilver in the moonlight. The wind shifted, and the wet-hay smell of horses hit her.

She leaned further out, and looked straight down. This was a mistake. She softly whispered a swear word,

and her stomach dropped down into her pelvis. She found herself retreating rather quickly, and digging her nails into the brickwork of the chimney stacks for reassurance. She had never been this high up, ever. The moon looked close enough to hit with a pebble.

Sophie peeled off her nightgown, and stood up in her knickers and vest. She spun on the spot, and the Paris sky spun in time with her. The wind blew stronger, and a great bubble of happiness was rising up through her chest into her nose. Sophie threw out her arms and danced a war dance round the chimneys, whooping, very quietly, under her breath.

Sophie would have liked to stay out all night, but sometime after the clocks struck two she grew cold and her knee began to bleed again. She wiped off the worst of the blood with leaves, and wrapped it more tightly with her stocking before she lowered herself through the skylight.

Just as her eyeline dropped down inside, she thought she saw something moving across the rooftop opposite. But night shadows, she knew, throw your eyes off-kilter, and it was just a large bird, or a swirl of night air.

CHAPTER TWELVE

Sophie did not sleep for long. She was only halfway through a dream when there was a clattering crash and a thump. Sophie jerked awake. She was lying face down, and her scream was muffled by her pillow; even so, a voice spoke very clearly in the darkness.

'Don't *wail* like that. You'll wake the whole hotel.'

Her dressing table was on the floor, next to a broken mug. Mud and soot was scattered across the carpet. And there was a boy standing at the foot of her bed.

The boy said, 'Stop it. *Arrête!* Stop crying! Stop, Sophie!'

Sophie had not been crying, in her own opinion; she had been choking, which seemed reasonable in the circumstances. She pushed the hair out of her eyes.

'Who are you?' She grabbed a book and held it over her heart. It might help if he tried to stab her. 'I'll scream.'

'No. Don't scream.'

'Why shouldn't I?' It was too dark to see him properly. 'I'm just about to.' He wasn't much older than she was, Sophie thought. He was long-legged, and his face was tight and wary, like an animal. He didn't look like a murderer. Her breath came a little more easily.

'Because I don't like screaming.'

'What do you want?'

'I want to talk to you, Sophie.'

'How do you know my name? And what are you doing here?'

'I heard the man saying it in the street. The long one. The one you called Charles. My name is Matteo,' he added, as an afterthought.

'You were watching us?'

The boy picked his nose. 'Yes. You're not special. I watch everybody.'

'And what if I scream for the police? What happens then?'

The boy shrugged. 'You won't. But if you do, I can be gone in …' He glanced, calmly measuring, at the skylight. 'Six seconds.'

'Not if I stop you.'

He shrugged again. 'You could try.'

'And what are you doing here?' Sophie sat up. She thought, *Hold steady.* It was lucky that her room was so small. If he tried to attack her, she could get out through the door in three steps.

'I came in from the roof.'

'Yes, I can see that!' The window was open wider than she had left it, and he had brought at least two

dozen pigeons' worth of droppings in with him. 'But *why*? Why didn't you come through the door?'

'Don't you lock it? That's dangerous. You should lock your door.'

'Yes, I do, actually – *so that people can't come in.*'

The boy shrugged again. It was difficult to see, in the dark, but he might have been laughing at her. It was not a friendly laugh.

Sophie said, 'And how did you get on to the roof in the first place? I thought the only way on to the roof was my skylight.'

'You thought there was only one way on to the rooftop? *Vraiment?* You really thought that?'

'Why are you laughing?'

'There's hundreds of ways on to any rooftop. I could have climbed the drainpipe.'

'Did you? I would have heard you, wouldn't I?'

'Probably.'

'Then how *did* you?'

'I jumped. From the roof next door.'

'You jumped?' Sophie tried to look casual. 'Isn't that dangerous?' Her casual face felt stiff.

'No. I don't know. Maybe. Most things are dangerous. Your eye is twitching.'

'Is it?' Sophie abandoned her casual face. 'Oh.'

'*Oui*. Anyway.' He looked at her, and his eyes were black and hard. 'I came to tell you to keep off my rooftop.'

Sophie was speechless. She had half-expected him to ask for money; or to try to steal her cello. She was so startled that she forgot to be frightened. She said, 'It's not your rooftop! How can it be?'

'All the rooftops between the river and the train station are mine. I did not give you permission to go up there.'

'But … rooftops don't belong to anybody. They're like air, and water. They're no man's land.'

'They're not. They're mine.'

'How? How are they yours?'

'They just are. I know them best.'

Sophie's face must have looked as unconvinced as she felt, because the boy scowled.

'I do!' he said. 'I know exactly which chimney pots

are going to fall next autumn; and which gutter-mushrooms you can eat. I bet you didn't even know that you can eat those mushrooms that grow in the gutters?' Sophie hadn't known that there were such mushrooms, so she said nothing.

'And,' said the boy, 'I know every single bird's nest my side of the city.'

'That doesn't make the rooftops yours.'

'They belong to me more than to anyone else. I live on them.'

'No, you don't. You can't. Nobody lives on houses. You live *in* them.'

'You don't know what you're talking about.' The boy glared at her. He thumped the wall, and his hand left a sooty mark. The forefinger on his right hand was missing its tip. 'Look, this is stupid: I don't want to hurt you, but you have to stay off the roofs, or I will –'

'Will what?'

'I will hurt you,' he said, as matter-of-fact as a man selling bread.

'But *why*? What are you talking about?'

'You won't be careful enough. You'll give me away. You have the streets. Use them.'

Outside, the clouds moved away from the moonlight, and the room filled briefly with night-glow. The boy's face was darkly tanned (or dirt, perhaps? she thought), and seemed to be made up of sharp angles and eyes.

'I can't stay off the roofs.' said Sophie. 'I need them.'

'Why?'

'I …' said Sophie. 'It's too hard to explain. They feel safe.' Sophie blushed as she said it. The boy snorted. 'I mean, they feel important.'

The boy said, 'So? *Et alors?*'

'I feel like I've been here before,' she said. 'I think they might be a clue.' She expected that he would relent. It was what you did: you gave in. Giving in was good manners.

But the boy only stared at her, unsmiling. '*Non.* Rooftops are not a *clue*; they're mine. You'd give me away. You'd be slow. If you're slow, people see you.'

'I'm not slow!'

He looked at her hands, her feet. 'You'd bleed too easily. You look soft.'

'I am *not* soft. Look! No, don't go – *look*.' Sophie held out her left hand, palm up. The fingertips were calloused from her cello strings. 'Do they look soft to you?'

'Yes. They do.'

Sophie could have screamed.

The boy said, 'And you'd be noisy.'

'How do you know? You don't know me.' It seemed too much for this boy to break into her room in the moonlight and start insulting her volume control.

'All pavement-people are noisy. You'd give me away. Or you'd fall, and people would come searching around and find us all. I mean, find me. No. You're not coming up here again.'

'You can't stop me.'

The boy sighed. He spoke like someone holding on to his temper by a thread. 'Fine! Just, stay on your own rooftop, then. Don't go near the edge. Stay low. Don't stay out after sunrise, or people will see you.

Don't make a noise, or I'll hear and I'll come and burn off all your hair while you're sleeping.'

'But I can't!' said Sophie. 'Really, I can't. I need to look around. I need to find out more. Couldn't –' She hesitated. 'Could I come with you?'

The look he gave her was cold as ice. It burned. 'Fine! If you can catch me.'

The boy hadn't been lying when he said he could be gone in six seconds. He gripped hold of the window frame, and had twisted himself up and out before Sophie had counted to five. He seemed made of springs and leather.

Sophie followed, with only a little scrabbling, a little blood. Her legs were long, and she was quick; but the boy, as she clambered on to the slate, was already four rooftops down the road. His run was lilting, and peculiar. At least, she thought it was him; she could see only a black shadow, mixing with the shadows cast by the clouds scudding across the moon.

Sophie set after him. The night had turned damp, and the slate was slippery in unexpected places. Sophie didn't dare follow fast; she jogged, as quickly

as she dared, across her own rooftop, and across the next.

Rooftop running was not like other running. Sophie tried to keep her head low, and her back half down. A bottom cropping up over the balustrades and chimney pots would be impossible to explain. Her arms and fingers seemed longer than usual, and got in the way.

Sophie halted, panting. The wind blew harder, and she gripped a chimney pot. Clocks below her began to strike four, and Paris was waking. Its sound was like the hum of a hundred secrets, she thought: it was the mutter of a dozen soothsayers.

But the boy was nowhere. The boy had disappeared.

CHAPTER THIRTEEN

The next night Sophie began training.

She worked harder than she had ever worked in her life. She did sit-ups, and pull-ups on the door-frame. She practised balancing on one leg with her eyes closed, again and again. Her first effort was seven seconds. Her hundredth was one minute and forty-two seconds. She ran barefoot back and forth across the rooftop, and sang under her breath to keep away the pain.

At about one in the morning, she realised quite suddenly what had made Matteo's run look different; it was toe first rather than heel first, which shifted your

centre of gravity, she found, to somewhere near the knees. The realisation was like hot water, like a maths problem solved.

At two in the morning, the boy appeared. He was two rooftops down, crouched behind the chimney pot. She saw him, but she didn't think he realised he had been spotted.

She shouted, 'I can see you! I'm not going to give in!' She turned a cartwheel. It was the most defiant cart-wheel ever to have been turned on a Paris rooftop.

Sophie spun on the spot. She felt on edge, and tough. It was unlikely, Sophie thought, that her muscles had grown stronger. She had a feeling that took months. It was more that she needed, now, to use them, and they had woken up for her. They felt as a cat's muscles feel: more twitching, and more ready.

Muscles, she thought, *are a thing worth having.* They make the world easier to reach.

The wind up here was strong, and chimney dust blew in her eyes. She looped back her hair with a twig.

The dark was darker up on the roof; it was thick and silent. Down on the street, the dark feels dull and matter-of-fact, like a blackboard. Up here, it felt full of unseen birds and city whispers. The smell, too, was different. From the street, she reckoned she could smell only a few metres' worth of smells. From up here, all the bakers and all the pet shops of Paris mixed their scents. The result was something thick and peculiar and delicious.

From the roof, the moon looks twice as large, three times as beautiful. The moon, seen from the rooftops, is a thing worth spending time on.

Sophie imagined her mother, up here, amongst the stars. Mothers belong on rooftops.

Sophie walked to the next rooftop, and then jumped the three-foot gap to the next, and ran another three rooftops. She shouted, 'Matteo! I know you can hear me. I won't give up! I'm going to keep exploring!' Then,

tentatively, feeling foolish, Sophie called into the night, 'Pax? Friends?'

Somewhere below her, a horse whinnied. It sounded as though it were laughing.

On the way back, she ran; ran properly, not a jog. Her heart was beating so fast that it was nudging against her bones. The wind pulled at her clothes and hair, but she stayed steady. She thought, *This is how heaven must feel.* She felt confident as a crow. *Say what you will against crows,* Sophie thought, *they do look like they know what they're doing.*

CHAPTER FOURTEEN

Sophie prepared for the meeting with the chief commissioner the way other people prepare for war. She washed with cold water, and smoothed her eyebrows with spit. She rubbed lavender against her wrists and neck. She practised an innocent expression in the mirror. She polished her shoes with spit, and washed the oil and bird droppings out of her stockings.

'You look,' said Charles, when they met at the front door, 'as though you're about to sing the solo in the church choir.'

'Do I?' She knotted the bottom of her plait, and tucked it under her hat. 'That's what I was hoping.'

'You do. You look as though you own a minimum of one pony. You look nothing like yourself. Well done.'

As they walked through the streets, Sophie felt she was looking at Paris with newly critical eyes. She kept her head tilted back, and almost without noticing, she judged the rooftops. That one would be too steep; and that one much too low; that one was perfect, except for the flimsy-looking drainpipe.

The police headquarters, she thought as they came in view of it, would be wonderful to climb. Its roof was flat, and its drainpipe was thick iron. She tensed as they went in. She would much rather be out on the rooftop than inside.

The meeting was held in a room with high ceilings and large furniture. It seemed designed to make

Sophie feel small. A guard stood to attention outside the door.

It became clear immediately that it was less of a meeting than an ambush.

The commissioner did not stand up to greet them. He waved at two seats. '*Bonjour.* Good day.' His accent was thickly French; it sounded moustachey.

'Please 'ave a seat, Mr Maxim, Miss Maxim.'

Sophie had sat before she realised what he had said. Then it hit her, and she leaped up and jumped towards the door. 'Charles!' she cried. 'Come on! Run!'

Charles hadn't moved. He stood in the centre of the room, holding his umbrella. His face was rigid. He looked like a soldier. Sophie stood with the doorknob in her hand.

The commissioner smiled. 'I could say, welcome to Paris, but I wouldn't mean it.'

'What's going on?' said Charles. 'Are you planning to arrest me?'

'*Non*. I am planning to give you a choice. Sit down.'

'What choice is that?' said Charles. He remained standing.

'Please sit down. You are wasting a good chair.'

Sophie stayed where she was. Charles sat. 'What choice was it you had in mind?'

'A very simple one. If you do not abandon your childish search and leave this country, I will 'ave you thrown in jail.' His nostrils widened as if in pleasure at the thought.

'I see. Well, that is admirably straightforward. May I ask why haven't you done so already?'

'I think we want to avoid fuss, *si possible. Non?*'

'No,' said Sophie. 'No, I'd rather have fuss. I need to find her.'

'Little girl.' He turned on her. All the wealth in the room seemed to mass itself behind him. '*Écoutez-moi.* Listen to me. The *Queen Mary* was a wreck. No women survived. The passenger lists, addresses, staff payrolls, insurance; it was all lost with the ship. I 'ave no wish to start an inquiry. You 'ave no wish to be in an orphanage. We are like twins, are we not?'

'I hate you,' whispered Sophie. 'I hate you.'

'I am giving you a day to book your passage back to England. I recommend the port at Dieppe. It's very fine this time of year.'

Charles bowed. 'You will notice that my young ward has not, as yet, spat on you. I admire her restraint.' For one mad moment Sophie thought Charles was going to spit on the man himself – he had his head thrown back, in spitting position – but he only took her hand, and led her from the room.

They walked down a hundred metres of corridor, until they were out of sight of the guard; then Charles swore, under his breath, and broke into a run. Sophie could only just keep pace with him. Her hat fell off, and she left it where it was. They burst through the grand doors, past the startled doorman, and out into the sunshine.

'I couldn't stand it in there a moment longer,' said Charles. 'He was lying.'

'Yes! His nostrils were flaring.'

'You saw it too. Flaring wide enough to fit a canal boat.'

'But I don't understand.' She stopped, and leaned against a lamp post. 'Why does he care? Do you think he had anything to do with it? With the ship?'

'Not with the ship, perhaps. But I think he may be suppressing the records.'

'Why? What do you mean? Why would they do that?'

'Ten years ago there was a scandal in Europe; a series of sunken ships. It was an insurance con: an ancient ship would be certified safe, it would sink, the insurance would be claimed. The survivors were told conflicting stories; the truth got blurred. Smudged. And the records would be burned or hidden, so that nobody could check who had certified the ship. There were eight cases, in all, before anyone was caught.'

'But … did people die?'

'Hundreds of people. It would have looked suspicious had they not.'

'That's disgusting! That's not human!'

'I know, my darling. Money can make people inhuman. It is best to stay away from people who care too much about money, my darling. They are people with shoddy, flimsy brains.'

'And … if the *Queen Mary* was one of those ships?'

'Yes?'

'Does that mean they will have burned the records?' They couldn't have, she thought. They mustn't. She needed them.

'Kept them, more likely. If more than one person was involved, it would be unwise to burn anything.'

'Why? I don't get that; I'd burn them, if it was me.'

'If you are caught, it is better to have proof you were not acting alone. Criminals are only loyal to each other in books.' Charles polished his glasses. Behind them, his eyes were grim. 'I'm not saying that's what happened. But it's possible.'

'And never ignore a possible?'

'Precisely.' He smiled a half smile. 'I couldn't have said it better myself.'

'Where would they keep papers like that?'

'It could be anywhere. In their homes, in their offices, under their floorboards. Or, there's an archive room on the top floor of the building. Four million sheets of paper in one hundred filing cabinets, I am told.'

'Who told you?'

'The young woman at the reception desk. Somebody should promote her. She's wasted on reception.'

They crossed the road, avoiding a gaggle of American tourists.

'Charles?'

'Yes?'

'Nothing, actually.' They walked on. Then, 'Charles?'

'I'm listening.'

'Wouldn't the best place to hide papers be with other papers?'

'Very possibly.'

'So –'

'Yes, I see what you mean.'

'And the archive's on the top floor?'

'Sophie –'

'That's what you said, wasn't it?' The tingle and twitch that come with an idea were prickling at her skin. 'What if –'

'No, Sophie.'

'But –'

'*No.* I am not having you caught. You're not going anywhere near the place. Don't even think of it.'

'But we're not actually going to go back to England, are we.' It was not a question. 'I won't. I *can't*. Not when we might be so close.'

'Of course not. But, Sophie – and I do mean this – you will have to stay inside the hotel.'

'But, you can't do it without me –'

'I can. You will have to trust me to go on without you.'

'But then how will I be able to help? You have to let me help! What are you going to do?'

'I'm going to get a lawyer, Sophie.'

'What kind of lawyer?'

'The best we can afford. Which isn't terribly good, I'm afraid. And I'll lurk in some of these bars, and see if I can pick up any gossip.'

'About my mother? About Vivienne?'

'About cellists of any kind, I think.'

'Oh.' Sophie was sceptical about lawyers in general, but Charles looked so determined and his eyes were so kind that she couldn't bear to tell him so. Instead she said, 'But if I could just get into the archive –'

'No. There's a guard on every floor. You saw the one outside the commissioner's office?'

'Yes. But, what if the archive –'

'The guard was built like a rhinoceros. There are men like him on every floor.' Charles glared into the sun. 'In fact, Sophie, I need you to keep away from the other hotel guests. Don't even open the door to your room.'

'Fine,' she said. She wasn't lying, she told herself. 'I won't even open the door.'

He looked at her, and she looked back, innocent-eyed.

'I'm sorry,' he said. 'I know it's stuffy in there. I'll bring you some good books.'

Sophie said nothing, but the flickering in her chest did not go away. *Never,* she thought, *ignore a possible.*

CHAPTER FIFTEEN

That night, Sophie said goodnight to Charles early, and clambered on to the rooftops the moment the sun had begun to set.

She sat against a chimney pot, and waited for it to become properly dark. While she waited, she tucked her knees under her chin, and tried to muster her options.

She was surprised to find that giving up was not one of them. It was odd. She wasn't, as far as she knew, brave. She was afraid of deep water and large crowds, and cockroaches. And when she thought of being caught and taken back to England she felt physically

sick with dread. And yet giving up felt as impossible as flying. Her mother felt so much more real, here. She could almost smell her; she would smell, Sophie felt sure, of roses, and resin. She felt just around the corner.

Sophie got to her feet. Sophie had not thought she had a plan; but she acted purposefully as if she had planned it all along. She pulled off her shoes and held them in her teeth. Then she headed north, in the direction of the boy.

After twenty minutes, she squatted on her heels, and fished the laces from one of her shoes. She tied it round the chimney pot. She wanted him to know that she was not afraid to leave her own rooftop. At each new roof Sophie tied something to the chimney pot: first her other shoe lace, and then her stockings and

two hair ribbons, all of which were easy to tie; and then her handkerchief, which was not quite large enough, and kept coming undone at the top. At the eighth rooftop, she wound her dressing gown round the chimney. It was grey with much washing, and she was not sorry to part with it.

At the ninth rooftop, Sophie came to a halt. She stood on one leg. There was a gap, as long as an ironing board, between her rooftop and the next. *It's not far,* she told herself. She would almost certainly make it. But, somehow, she couldn't persuade her feet to agree.

Sophie hesitated. Then she tugged off her nightdress and threw it on to the rooftop. There was one second when she thought it was going to drop straight down the chimney. Instead it landed neatly on the edge and lay there, its arm waving in the breeze, as if it were saluting the dark.

Then Sophie turned and ran, as swift as she dared, dressed only in her pants and with her shoes in her mouth and her arms out for balance, back along the slate, back along the tip-tops of the city, over

the heads of a hundred dreaming Frenchmen, and back to bed.

Matteo appeared the next night, carrying her nightdress and stockings. He came at the stroke of midnight, under cover of the chiming clocks. Sophie didn't wake until he was standing three inches from her face.

'My God!' she said. 'You startled me.'

'I know.' He dumped the clothes on her bed. 'I kept the dressing gown,' he said. 'I wanted it.' He sat on the edge of her bed. 'You might as well explain,' he said.

Sophie said, 'Do you swear not to tell anybody?'

'No,' said the boy.

Nobody ever said no. Sophie stared. 'You don't?'

'I never swear anything. Tell me anyway.'

Sophie bit her lip; but the boy looked fearless. Fearless people are not usually telltales.

'If you tell on me,' she said, 'I'll come after you. Remember, I'm not frightened of rooftops.'

She told him everything. She started with the

Queen Mary, and worked through Miss Eliot and Charles, and her cello, and finished here, in Paris, amongst the chimney pots. 'And the thing is, it feels like I've been here before,' she finished.

'In Paris?'

'In Paris, *and* on the rooftops. But it's so difficult,' she said. 'Charles tries, but he's just one person. And nobody else will help me.'

'Is that a request?'

She looked at the boy. He seemed to be wearing two pairs of shorts, one on top of the other. The red pair on top was missing half the left leg and the blue pair showed through. Together they just about made up one pair of shorts. His jersey was threadbare, but his face, she thought, was not. His face was sharp and clever.

She said, 'Yes. It is.'

'Do you have a plan?'

'Of course. I'm going to make posters. And, there's the lawyers.'

Matteo snorted. 'They won't help you.'

'Yes, they will! Why would you say that?'

'You might find one, I suppose. But I don't think

anyone will take on the commissioner of police. All the lawyers in Paris are corrupt, and most of the policemen.'

'How do you know?' Sophie's heart felt suddenly grey. 'You can't know that! Someone's *got* to help! It's wildly important.'

'I listen to people all day. I live on top of the law courts, so I do know.'

'But you can't hear anything from a rooftop!'

'I can. Where I live, I can hear half of the city. It's like a wind tunnel; I can hear all the music in Paris, and all the horses, and all the crime.'

Sophie froze. 'You can hear all the music?'

'Yes. Of course.'

'What music do you hear?'

'All sorts. Women singing, mostly. And men with guitars, and the soldiers' band.'

'Do you hear cello music? Do you hear Fauré's *Requiem*?'

'I wouldn't recognise a requiem,' said Matteo. 'What is it? It sounds like a skin infection.'

'I can play it for you.' Sophie leaped up to fetch her

cello. Then she hesitated. 'If I play now, people will hear. They might come up and find you.'

'Come outside, then. I'll go first and you can pass up your … cello, is the word, yes?'

Outside, she sat on the chimney pot, and set her cello between her legs. She knew the *Requiem*, but she had never played it double time.

'It won't be perfect, all right? But I think it was something like this. Listen carefully, all right? And tell me if you've ever heard it.' Sophie stumbled over the fingering, but she thought it sounded at least something like the magic Monsieur Esteoule had played. When she had finished, Matteo shrugged.

'Possibly.'

'Possibly what?'

'*Possibly* I've heard it. What did you say?'

'Nothing.' In fact she had whispered, 'Never ignore a possible.' But she hadn't meant him to hear.

He said, 'I'm not good at music. Unless it's birds. You'd have to come and listen yourself.'

'Can I? Really? When?'

He snorted again. 'Whenever you like. I don't have a busy diary.'

'Tomorrow?'

'*D'accord.*'

'I don't speak French.' But his face had seemed to say, yes.

'I said, fine. I'll come and fetch you.'

'At midnight?' she asked. It had begun to rain. Matteo ignored it.

'*Non.* It's not dark enough at midnight. Two-thirty. Don't fall asleep. And wear something warm. It can be windy, up high.'

'Yes, of course!' The rain grew heavier. 'Wait a second. Rain isn't good for the wood.' Sophie lowered her cello back into her bedroom. When she turned back, Matteo had vanished.

Back inside, Sophie pulled the window shut, and huddled into the warm patch in her bed, but she did not fall asleep again until dawn. She lay listening to the rain blowing against the glass. Her heart was dancing double time.

CHAPTER SIXTEEN

If she had obeyed Charles and stayed in her room all day and all night, Sophie would, she thought, have gone straightforwardly crazy. She tried to reassure herself that she was not breaking any rules. She was not opening the door to her bedroom. The thought of the rooftops kept her steady during the day. Sophie counted the hours until sunset.

By nightfall it had grown cold, and Sophie put on her two pairs of stockings under her nightdress. She hadn't packed enough warm clothes, so she pulled the pillowcases off the pillows and knotted them together to make a scarf. It felt limp and not entirely comfortable,

but she thought it was preferable to nothing. Then she got into bed, and wedged her hairbrush behind her neck so she wouldn't fall asleep, and waited.

Matteo arrived as the clocks struck the half hour. He knocked on the skylight, and then stood impatiently flicking pebbles down into her room until she climbed out.

'Hello,' said Sophie. '*Bonsoir.*'

'*Oui, bonsoir.*' He wore a pack on his back, and his shorts had been swapped for a pair of trousers. They looked like they had been in a fight, and lost. He said, 'You're learning French?'

'A little.' Sophie flushed. 'It's not easy.'

'Yes it is. I know dogs that speak French. I know *pigeons.*'

'That's different.'

'How? How is it different?'

'Well, I'm not a pigeon.' A thought struck her. 'How long did it take you to learn English? Do all French people speak it like you do?'

'*Je ne sais pas*. I always knew it, a little. There's a bar where the English diplomats go. It has a courtyard. I can hear them speaking from my rooftop. And I learned to read it while I was in –' He stopped.

'While you were where?'

'In an orphanage.' He shook his head, as if clearing water from his ears, and changed the subject, 'Listen – I meant to ask – where I live is one of the tallest buildings in Paris. Are you afraid of heights?'

'No, I don't think so. I mean, I'm up here, aren't I?'

'This isn't high! This is practically pavement. I mean, are you good with *real* heights?'

'I'm not bad,' said Sophie. She cast her eyes down at the slate.

'Oh.'

'Quite good, I think.'

'Then you can't come. Quite good isn't good enough. Sorry.' He turned to go.

'Wait! I was being modest!'

'But you just said –'

'I'm very good,' said Sophie. 'I'm brilliant at them.' Matteo was obviously not the sort of boy who understood modesty, and she could not risk being left behind. 'Brilliant,' she said again.

'You shouldn't say what you don't mean, then. Are you ready?'

'Yes.' It seemed wise to change the subject. 'Whereabouts do you live?' said Sophie. 'Near here?'

'Yes. But not on this street. This street is too poor.'

'Is it? Oh.' It looked quite grand, to Sophie, with its tall lamp posts and elegant thin streets. 'Why does that matter, anyway?' She looked at his clothes, and at the mud clinging to the tips of his hair at the front. 'I wouldn't have thought you'd be a snob.'

'Lots of reasons.' Matteo looked haughty.

'Like what, though? Please? I'm curious.'

'Poor buildings are usually pointed; rich buildings are usually flat. Pointed roofs are no good. Poor buildings are … unpredictable. You can't be sure if you're going to put your foot through the slate. And they're too low. In the … *ach, banlieues* … the suburbs, I think you say? Where there are just houses: no offices, no churches? I never go there: the buildings are too low.'

'Really? Always?'

'Almost always. It's like people; rich buildings are tall, poor buildings are stunted.'

'Why does that matter?'

'Why do you think?'

Sophie stared out across the rooftops. 'Because with small buildings they can see you from the street?'

'*Oui*. Otherwise, I can go almost everywhere. At night. Never during the day.'

'Do you go to the parks?' *It's what I would do*, she thought, *if I could*.

'*Non*. Of course not.'

'Why not? It would be wonderful to have a park to yourself. And there'd probably be food.'

'I never go on the ground. Not for years. You can't get trapped on a rooftop.'

Sophie blinked. 'Never?' It sounded impossible. 'But what if you need to cross a road? Between rooftops?'

'I go by trees. Or on top of the lamp posts.'

'And you never just … cross a road?'

'*Non*.'

'Why not?'

'It's dangerous,' he said.

'Oh …' Matteo's voice was sounding increasingly curt. But she couldn't hold it back. 'You know, most people would say it's the other way around.'

'Most people are stupid. It's easy to be caught on the ground. Everyone gets caught.'

'Caught?' Sophie tried to decipher his face in the darkness. He looked serious. 'Is somebody looking for you?'

Matteo ignored that. 'So, you want to see where I live, or no?'

'Yes! Now?'

'Now!' And without looking behind to see if she was following, Matteo took off.

When Matteo was standing still, he was quite an unusual-looking person. When he moved, he was astonishing. He seemed made of India rubber. He ran low, and used his hands as though they were extra feet. She followed as quietly and quickly as she could,

tripping over the rough slate. Quite a lot of the skin of her knees got left behind.

Matteo ran for ten minutes, and Sophie followed, balancing along the tips of slanted rooftops, sprinting along the flat ones, and jumping the small gaps between them. Twice, as the buildings grew taller, Matteo showed her how to clamber up a length of drainpipe to reach the next roof.

'The thing about drainpipes,' he said, hanging upside down from one of them, 'is that you mustn't put your foot through a window while you're pulling yourself up. People tend to notice that.'

Sophie tackled the drainpipes without talking. Her nails scraped against the metal horribly, but otherwise they were not so different from trees. When she thumped down on to the slate beside Matteo, he nodded. He almost smiled. 'Not bad,' he said. 'Next time, keep your knees in. It makes it easier to grip. But that was good. At least, good-ish.'

Sophie flushed with pleasure. Matteo ran on. Below their feet, Paris slept.

They were reaching an area full of flags and vast

solemn-looking buildings. As the rooftops got wider and larger, Matteo went faster. Once, on the fiddly roof of some kind of chapel, Sophie stumbled, and her stomach inverted. She clutched the cross for balance, and stopped to catch her breath.

The wind was high, and across the road, a shadow was swinging by its knees from the top of the lamp post.

Sophie saw it. She definitely saw it. But by the time she had untangled her hair from her face and could see again, the girl had gone.

It took her a few minutes to catch up with Matteo. 'Matteo! Did you see her? The girl? Who was it?'

'I didn't see it. It will have been just nothing. A paper bag.'

'It was bigger than a paper bag. It was a girl!'

'A broken kite, maybe. A pillowcase. Come on.' He cracked his knuckles, and ran on.

It was ten minutes before Matteo again stopped. They were a jump across from a tall, curved rooftop. It gleamed greenish in the moonlight.

'Stay there.' Matteo jumped, then bent and rapped

lightly on the rooftop. It echoed. 'Copper,' he said. 'Take off your shoes before you come. Jump as softly as you can.'

Sophie pulled off her shoes. 'What shall I do with them?'

'Here; throw your shoes to me. *Ach*, I hate copper.'

Sophie did so. Thank goodness, she thought, that Charles had taught her to throw.

'What's the worst kind of rooftop?' she asked. 'Is it copper?'

'*Non*. Stone tiles; the old ones, from the old days. They're quieter than copper, but too easy to … what's the word? Topple?'

'Dislodge?' Sophie held her breath and eyed the gap. It was no wider than her arm, but even so it made her shiver. She jumped, landing messily, but leaped straight to her feet.

'Maybe. Yes, dislodge. And flat rooftops are best.' He handed back her shoes. 'Anything with big slabs is good. Stone, or slate, or metal.'

'Right. Like on the Hotel Bost?'

'Yes. And on most state buildings; you know,

hospitals, prisons. Theatres are good. And cathedrals. But anything four floors or under is too low to sleep on. They can see you from the street if you roll too near the edge. Wait, don't put your shoes back on. Tie them round your waist.'

'All right.' Sophie wound her shoe laces round her waist. 'Why, though?' She arranged the shoes carefully, so that one hung over each hip.

Matteo said, 'You need your toes, up here. You shouldn't ever wear shoes.'

'But don't you –'

'People think toes are useless. That's because they're stupid.'

'But don't your feet get –'

His face took on an aggravating, headmaster look. 'You thought toes were only good for collecting dirt, *non*?'

'Not exactly, but –'

'But nothing. Toes are life and death. You need toes for balance. I've broken every toe at least twice. Look.' Matteo held up a foot.

It was black. The base of his foot was calloused over.

Not one inch of soft skin was visible. He tapped the bottom. 'You hear? It's like tin. You could play music on my feet.'

Sophie said, 'But don't they get cold in winter?'

'Yes.'

'Oh.' Sophie waited for him to say more. He didn't. She said, 'But couldn't you wear shoes, when you're just on your own rooftop? I could give you mine, if you like. I've got two pairs.'

'*Non, merci.*'

'They're not girly.' Sophie held up the shoes hanging round her waist. 'They're like these ones: boys' boots. They were a present from Charles. What size are your feet?'

'You can't wear shoes up here. You never know when you might need to run.'

'But what about when it *snows*?'

'In winter, to stay warm, I wrap my ankles and calves with goose fat and bandages, and feathers between the layers. So it's almost like having shoes, but it leaves your toes free.'

'Oh. Does that work?'

'No. But, almost.'

'Why goose fat?'

He shrugged. 'Fat keeps you warm. Goose fat is best, but you can use pigeon, if you have to. Sparrows don't have enough fat on them. Squirrel meat's too dry. You need something greasy.' Without her permission Sophie's face formed an *ugh*. He saw, and scowled. 'I never said it was nice, but it helps. Let's go. Are you ready?'

Sophie checked the laces round her waist were tightly knotted. Then, 'Matteo?' she said. 'Where did you learn all this?'

'Accidentally, mostly. Practice.' Matteo lifted his shirt. A purplish scar ran from his belly button to his ribcage. 'Trial and error.'

'My God! How did you do that?'

'Falling. On a weathervane. And this one –' he showed her a bruise, still a fresh green, on his shoulder – 'was when I fell on to a chimney pot.'

'Does it hurt?'

'Of course.' He shrugged. 'We bleed more often than most people. It's not the end of the world.'

'Oh.' Then she said, 'Matteo?'

'Quoi?'

'Who is we?'

The look in his face was so different, so suddenly, that Sophie stepped back. 'Me,' he said. 'I said me.'

Matteo took off again. This time, when he reached the gaps between rooftops, he jumped without waiting for her or looking back. Sophie had to stop to gather her courage before each one; they would have been nothing on the ground, but up high they took all the nerve she had. Soon she was a roof's length behind.

'Can we slow down, please? Just a little?'

'*Non*,' said Matteo. He pushed his hair from his eyes in order to glare at her, and sped up.

After half an hour, Matteo did slow. When he turned to face her, he seemed to have regained his temper. He said, 'This is the last gap. It's the next building.'

By now Sophie felt like an old hand. 'Do we jump?' She pushed back her hair and crouched.

'*Non! Arrête!* Sophie! Stop!'

'What? What's wrong?'

'You can't jump on to that roof. It's a … I don't know the word – a crumbler?'

'What do you mean?'

'The parapet is too old to jump on to. The tiles snap off.'

'Oh. Goodness.' Sophie stared at the gap. It wasn't very wide, it was true: but it was a long drop to the ground.

'I know! It's so good. It's why I chose to live here: it means nobody can follow, unless they know. If you were to jump without knowing, you'd die, I think.'

'Do you realise that's not very reassuring?'

It was dark, but she thought Matteo smiled. 'I don't bother too much about reassuring.'

Sophie realised she'd been holding her breath. She gulped in air. It was surprising what a difference oxygen made to bravery. 'How do you get across?' she asked.

'It's easy. You step.'

Jumping was one thing. It was a rush and a gasp and it lit up your insides. Slowly stepping across nothingness was quite another. She tried to imagine it. 'I can't.

I'll have to jump it,' she said. Terror rose up in Sophie's throat. It tasted green. 'That's too wide to step.'

'*Non*, not for you. Your legs are like drainpipes.'

'They're not.'

'That was a compliment! You were born for rooftops. And anyway, legs stretch wider than you think.'

'I just don't know if I can.'

'You said you were good at heights.'

'I am!' How *dare* he, Sophie thought. 'We've come miles! And I'm covered in blood and soot and I didn't stop once.'

'So? It doesn't count if you don't get to the end.' He laid a hand on her shoulder.

Sophie leaped away. 'Don't you dare push me!' Matteo was unpredictable. It occurred to her for the first time that rooftops and unpredictable people are a dangerous mix.

'I wasn't going to!' he hissed. 'And keep your voice down.'

'Sorry. I'm sorry.' She peered over the edge again. 'OK. Tell me what we do. I'm not saying I'll do it, though.'

'OK. First, you close your eyes,' said Matteo.

'Matteo. We're on a *rooftop*.'

'Close your eyes. If you keep them open, you'll look down, and if you look down, you'll fall.'

'Oh.' Sophie closed them. 'Ah.'

'I'm going to lead you to the edge. Are your eyes closed?'

'Yes.' In fact, Sophie was peering down under her lashes. She could see her bare feet approaching the edge.

'No, they're not. Close them properly. It will be easier, I promise you. *Et maintenant* – I hold the back of your nightdress, so you can't fall – and you take a step.'

'How big?'

'About the length of a pig.'

The length of a pig, thought Sophie. She was going to die because she had never looked properly at a pig.

'You'll be fine. You're safe.' Matteo sounded unusually serious. 'Keep your eyes shut.'

Sophie extended one leg into the gap. 'They're shut,' she said, and this time it was true. Gripping on to his arm, she stuck her leg out into nothing. It waved

around; and still it met nothing. Sophie shot her leg back, and stepped away from the edge.

'That's wider than a pig, Matteo!'

'The *length* of a pig. Pigs are quite long. Shake out your leg. I've got you. Try again. Further! Yes!' Sophie was almost doing the splits when her foot connected with the far edge.

'Now what?' She tried not to sound panicky, but her weight had shifted to somewhere over her knees, too far forward to pull it back, and she felt she might twist backwards into nothing any second. And if anyone was walking in the tiny alley beneath they would be able to see her pants up her nightdress. *This is why everybody should wear trousers,* she thought. *This.*

'Now you let go of me,' Matteo said, 'And –'

'What? No! Don't you –'

'Just for a second –' Matteo had already detached himself, 'and I step ...' There was the lightest of thumps. A squirrel would have made more noise.

'And you give me your hand.'

Sophie did so, and blushed. It was slippery with sweat.

'And I pull you over.' His tug was startlingly strong, and she was dragged, shoulders and arms and knees all together, across the gap.

'And now,' said Matteo, 'you stand up. And you wipe your hands.' He grinned. 'You could water plants with your palms. Come on. We're almost there.'

'You said this was the last one! You said this was it!'

'*Oui*. I lied.'

CHAPTER SEVENTEEN

Matteo straightened the bag on his back, and beckoned her along the rooftop. 'When the moon comes out, you'll be able to see.' He pointed, and puffed out his chest. 'There – that rooftop there – that's where I live.'

'It's very nice,' Sophie said, politely. Her eyes were shut, but it was what you were supposed to say when people show you their homes.

'Very nice? That's all?'

'Sorry.' Sophie had been gathering together her breath and her courage. She opened her eyes; and then opened them again, wider. 'You live *there*?'

It was beautiful. It was the same dizzying height as the building they were sitting on, but it was built of sandstone, and in the moonlight it glowed yellow. Statues of warriors and women were carved into the walls. It looked like there would be chandeliers inside, and men with power at their fingertips. At the top, a French flag flew from a polished silver pole.

'It's the law court,' said Matteo. 'It's the most important building in Paris.'

'You sound like an estate agent.'

'It's *true*!' He looked furious. 'It's the most beautiful building in Europe. It says so in the guidebooks.'

'How do we get there?' The gap between their building and Matteo's home was too wide to jump. No tree could possibly reach as high.

'If I was alone, I'd go round the back, up the oak

and then the drainpipe.' Matteo took off his backpack. 'But the jump from the tree to the pipe takes practice. See?' He rolled back his sleeve. A scar ran from his wrist to the crook of his elbow. 'The painful kind of practice.' He opened his pack. 'I brought this, instead.'

'Rope?' Sophie looked at the thick coil in Matteo's hand. It was a good length. Rope is heavy; Matteo must have been stronger than he looked. 'What's the hook on the end for?'

'You'll see in a second.'

'Are we going to climb? Is that what the rope's for?' Sophie tried not to let the fear in her chest become audible. Matteo, she thought grudgingly, must have been born with a larger than usual portion of courage.

'I said, you'll see.' Matteo walked to the very edge of the building and curled his toes over the edge. Sophie's stomach gave a swoop of protest, but he seemed as cool as if he was standing on the edge of the kerb. 'Stand back,' he said. He whirled the rope above his head, spat over the edge of the roof, and let the rope fly. It hooked on to the bracket holding up the drainpipe on the other side.

Matteo gave it a tug. His face had the same listening expression that Charles had around music.

'That'll be fine,' he said. He pulled it taut, and tied the end in his hand to a hooked nail in the wall. He spat on the knot for luck.

'Now, we walk,' he said.

Sophie stared at him. 'You're joking.'

'You said you wanted to see where I live. This is how you get there. It's easy!'

'It's *string*! A piece of string between the sky and the pavement. *String*, Matteo.'

'Rope.'

From here, Sophie thought, it definitely looked like string. It looked impossible.

Matteo's face, in the dark, was exasperated. 'If you want, you could try to jump from the tree to the pipe, but that would be stupid. This is safer.'

'A tightrope.' It was almost invisible from where Sophie stood; just a slither of grey in the darkness. 'A *tightrope* is your safer option.'

Matteo looked coldly at her over the gap. 'If you don't do it, I won't help you. Cowards don't deserve help.'

'Don't call me a coward. I'm not a coward.'

'*Oui, je sais.*'

'What?'

Matteo shrugged, half apologetic. 'I don't necessarily think you're a coward.'

'Then don't say it, ever again.'

'Look, this is easy. I'll show you.'

Matteo spat again, and blew his nose with his thumb. He stepped on to the rope. For one second he hesitated, swaying, and then he paced, foot over foot, until he was right in the middle of the rope. His arms were stretched out. Like wings, Sophie thought. His upper body moved in time with the breeze, and he looked like he was balancing on thin air. The wind ruffled his clothes and flipped his hair on end.

It was the most unexpected thing in the world, she thought. It took the breath out of her.

Very slowly, he turned – Sophie's throat tightened in terror, but the boy gave not a single wobble – and he walked back to her. 'Coming?' he said. He held out one hand.

The thing that amazed Sophie was that she didn't

even have to consider. Perhaps because it was so beautiful. Perhaps because sometimes everybody needs to be stupidly and recklessly brave.

'Yes,' Sophie said. 'I'm coming.'

She walked to the edge of the roof. That was easy. She curled her toes on the parapet, and looked down. That was not so easy. Her hands were hot. *Hold steady*, she thought.

'Slowly,' said Matteo. 'You start slowly. Can you put one foot on the rope?'

Sophie felt it sharp and springy beneath her bare foot. 'Oh my *heart*, Matteo!' There was a whirlwind in her chest.

'Give me both your hands. I do the balancing for both of us, *oui*?'

'*Oui,*' said Sophie. 'Yes.'

'Other foot.'

Sophie's right foot left dry land. She stepped out over the air. '*Oh,*' she breathed. 'I think you must be mad. We must both be mad. Oh, God.'

'Good,' said Matteo. She wobbled, and he steadied her. 'Mad is good. Don't look down.'

'But then how do I know where to put my feet?' Sophie's voice came out higher than usual.

'You hold on to me; hold on to my shoulders. I'll go backwards. I'm doing all the balancing, OK? You just don't look down. Can you feel the rope with your feet?'

'Yes,' said Sophie. She dug her thumbs into his skin. 'Yes.'

'Now,' said Matteo. 'Left foot. Right. Grip with your toes. Left. Stop. Do *not* look down. Look up. At the top of my head. Can you feel the balance?'

Sophie's feet tickled against the prickle of the rope. 'I think so. Yes. Maybe.'

'*Bien,*' he said. He felt frighteningly thin and light. She thought his collarbone must be hollow, like a bird's. 'Keep breathing. Step.' Halfway along, he slowed and stopped.

'Why are you stopping?' said Sophie. She tried to keep the rasp of fear out of her voice. 'I think I'd rather we kept moving.'

'So you can look. See, Sophie! Don't look down – look across. There is all of Paris!'

Sophie looked, and gasped. Below her feet, Paris

stretched out towards the river. Paris was darker than London: it was a city lit in blinks and flickers. And it was Fabergé-egg beautiful, she thought. It was magic-carpet stuff.

'See? Best city in the world,' said Matteo. 'You will never feel as much like a king as up here.'

It was better than being a king. Kings, thought Sophie, would have bruised fingers from a thousand daily handshakes. This was like being a warrior, a sprite, a bird.

Far away, by the river, she thought she could see the Hotel Bost, and her own skylight.

'I wonder if I've left my candle burning,' she said. 'I think I can see it.'

Matteo ignored that. His face was whiter than usual, and his eyes brighter. He seemed to be listening to the rope. He said, 'Shall we feed the birds?'

'Yes.' Then a gust of wind tugged at her nightdress, and Sophie changed her mind. 'Or, no. No, actually, I think I'd rather keep going,' she said. 'Please!'

'*Ach, non!* To feed the birds while you are in the sky! This is a thing even a king cannot do.'

'But it's past midnight. The birds –' the rope gave a wobble, and a globule of something bitter rose up in Sophie's throat – 'the birds will be asleep.'

'They're just dozing. They'll wake if I call them. Just two minutes more, Sophie! I have hold of you. You can't fall if I have hold.'

'Quickly, then, OK?'

'You have to let go of me with one hand. I have grain, in my pocket; I'll put it in your palm. Yes? I have the balance, Sophie. You just keep your legs straight. *No, don't look down.*'

Sophie tried to take the grain from his hand without looking down at it. She failed. The whole world swooped. She could feel half of the grain slithering through her sweaty fingers. Her knees gave a spasm and the rope shuddered. 'Matteo! Help me.'

Matteo had never looked more calm. He said, 'Steady.' He tightened his grip on her, and shifted their balance. 'Are you panicking?'

'No,' lied Sophie.

'If you start to fall, I'll stop you. You understand, *oui*?

Yes? I have never fallen from a tightrope. At least, not far. Not *very* far, anyway. Breathe, please.'

'I am! Stop telling me to breathe!' The rope dug into the soles of her feet. 'I am breathing!'

Matteo said, 'Just one more minute. Unlock your knees. Good. I'm going to call the birds.'

'Matteo, I think I want to get off.' Sophie tried not to think of fifty-foot drops. She was not successful. 'Please, let's just get to the other end.'

'*Non*. Just one minute.' Matteo whistled: a scale of three notes, rising. It was sharp and clean and it rang out through the silent dark for miles. It cut through Sophie's panic. It sounded like rain coming.

He said, 'Can you whistle?'

'Yes.' There was a wind, and the rope swayed under her. Sophie shut her eyes.

'Copy me, then.'

Sophie gripped the rope with her toes. She whistled. It was like playing the cello; it made the rest of the world recede.

'That's good.' He sounded surprised. '*C'est très bien*. You didn't tell me you could do that.'

'Thank you.' She whistled again. It calmed her breath. She tried to make her throat vibrate, like the nightingales did.

'Open your eyes.' Matteo was grinning. She hadn't ever seen him smile like that. 'Look up!' he said.

Sophie looked up. Three birds were circling above Matteo's head.

'They know me, you see,' said Matteo. 'Hold out your seed. Higher than that. It has to be higher than your shoulder, or they'll try to crawl up your arm and on to your head.'

A bird landed on her hand, then a second one.

'*Oh!*' she breathed. They were heavy; their weight on her arms was the oddest delight. Their claws pinched at her skin. 'Hello,' she breathed. '*Bonsoir*.' The rope swayed under her feet as the second bird settled on her wrist.

Matteo shifted their balance. His face was muddy, but the pure white concentration showed through.

'They like you,' said Matteo. 'Look!'

Sophie looked. One of the pigeons was shifting and

flapping, up along her forearm towards her shoulder. It was as if it was testing her strength, she thought.

'Please stay,' she whispered to the birds. The birds seemed to approve of her. 'Don't go. Stay.'

The largest one pecked at the seed – which must have tasted rather sweaty by now, she thought – from the grooves in her palm.

Matteo whistled again, and another bird circled down, and landed on her head. Then a red-eyed dove landed on Matteo's shoulder, and pecked at the back of his neck.

'I know this one,' said Matteo. 'He's called Elisabeth.'

'He?'

'He's old. I met him when I was just a baby. I didn't know how to tell the sex, then; I thought he was a girl.'

'He's beautiful.'

'Yes, I know. I didn't think he'd come. He doesn't like strangers.' Elisabeth left Matteo and flapped on to Sophie's collarbone. It looked her in the eye. It bobbed its head. 'He must think he knows you.'

'Maybe he does!'

'He can't, though, can he? Silly Elisabeth.'

Elisabeth flapped his wings against her cheek, but did not take off. *To be approved by birds!* thought Sophie. *To be up in the centre of the sky!*

'Matteo! This is too good!' She couldn't think of words. 'This is like music.'

The city, Sophie thought, was different to what she had believed. 'It is kinder than you think,' she whispered. A blue tit landed on her hand. Sophie felt bejewelled. A blue tit is better than a ring. It pecked at her earlobe. 'It is wilder than you think.'

CHAPTER EIGHTEEN

It was half an hour before Sophie would let Matteo lead on to the other side. It was only the threat of the rising sun that made her give in. As soon as Matteo had backed on to the roof, and tugged her after him, Sophie's legs started to shake. She staggered three steps towards the centre and collapsed.

'Are you all right?' said Matteo. 'Do you need help?'

'No, I think *I'm* fine; it's just my legs that aren't.' She poked her calf muscle, and it gave a spasm. 'I think they'll be normal again in a second. I'll just sit here, if that's all right.'

'You're an odd colour. Do you want to sleep for a minute? I have a blanket. Or, it's a sack, but –'

'No, I couldn't sleep. I'll just sit.'

'Right. I'll make a fire.'

'Where? Here?'

'Of course not! Don't be stupid. It has to be by the chimney stack, so the smoke looks like it comes from the chimney. You stay there. Don't go anywhere.'

It was a few minutes before her legs would let her stand up and look around. The rooftop was large as a town square, and smooth slate. Sophie stamped, tentatively. Her legs seemed solid again. A plume of smoke rose from the centre of the roof. Sophie walked – or rather, limped – towards it.

Matteo was squatting behind the chimney stack,

feeding a fire with wood. From the look of it, it had once been a chair. He wore a sack over his shoulders.

'Matteo!' Sophie's eyes widened. 'Is this all yours?' She hoped he wouldn't be able to see in the dark how impressed she was.

'Of course. Who else's?' At Matteo's feet was a pile of arrows, tied in bundles. Neatly stacked against the chimney there was a pile of apples, a tin saucepan and a kettle, a heap of rough-cut wooden spoons, glass jars filled with nuts. There were two sacks; Sophie peeked inside. One was filled with leaves, and another filled with bones.

'Here. Sit.' He handed her a cushion.

'Did you make this?' It was sacking on the outside, but soft and thick.

'Of course.'

'What's it made of?' Sophie kneaded it. It was softer than anything they had at home. 'What's the stuffing?'

'It's just pigeon … *ach*, fluff. I don't know the word.'

'Down?'

'*Non*, not down. Down is like … not up. That soft white you get under the pigeon feathers, you know?

But,' he said, 'I use the outer feathers too, of course. I use everything. Even the bones.'

'You don't let them go when you've taken their feathers?'

'Let them go? Of course I don't let them go. I mean … they're dead. I don't pluck living pigeons. That would be very difficult for me and very confusing for the pigeon.'

'So you eat them?'

'Yes. I cook them and I eat them.' He took out a knife and held it out to her. 'With this. Sometimes, if it's raining and I'm hungry enough, I skip the cooking.'

'Do you eat the bones?'

'I boil them for soup.'

'Is it nice?'

'*Non.* It's disgusting. It's like glue. But it's better than nothing.'

'And the outer feathers? What do you do with them?' He was such a peculiar creature that she would not have been surprised if he had worn them, as a cloak. She would not have been surprised, in fact, if he had sewn them into wings.

'Look. That. There. No, *there*.'

Further along the roof, stretched between the two chimney stacks, there was a sheet. Sophie jogged over to look more closely. It was sewn with layer upon layer of pigeon feathers. It was oddly greasy, but beautiful. Under it was a bed made of sacks. She kneaded the mattress. It was the same soft down as her cushion.

'The feathers are waterproof,' said Matteo. She had not heard him come up behind her. 'It works like a tent. Only it was free.'

It wouldn't be warm, thought Sophie. It would be no real protection from the wind. 'Matteo, what do you do in winter? How do you stay warm?'

'I don't.' He shrugged. 'You get used to it. You don't get to like it.'

'Couldn't you go to the orphanage? Just for the winter?'

'No.'

'But –'

'I did, once. There was a fight, on a rooftop in the north, and I got cut. A bad one. It turned septic.' As he spoke, he tucked his right hand under his left

armpit. 'I thought I had no choice.' Matteo poked the fire too hard. It sparked, and Sophie ducked. He said, 'There were iron bars on the windows. I can pick a lock, but nobody can pick an iron bar.'

'But why would there be bars? Did people try to break in?'

'*Non*. Children tried to break *out*. But once they know you exist, they don't let you leave. It's illegal to be homeless in France, did you know that?'

Sophie hadn't known. It sounded the craziest law in the world. 'But you left, didn't you?'

'Yes. Through a chimney. I should never have gone in the first place. They're still looking for me; for me, and for some others. They put notices of runaways in the post offices, did you know *that*?'

'But why? Why did you run away, I mean? What happened?'

'Nothing. Nothing happened. It was like hell: the same thing every day. They shouted if we talked to each other at meals. They shouted if we laughed.'

'Really?' Sophie was stunned. 'I mean, literally?'

'*Oui*. You have no idea, Sophie. It was like being

nailed shut. I can't risk going on the ground again. It is better for people not to know I exist.' He turned away, and ran a twig under his toenails.

Sophie wasn't stupid. She turned back to the feather tent. 'Well, I think this is wonderful, up here! I think I'd never leave this rooftop, if I was you.' She stroked the feathers. Water lay in droplets on them, but the slate underneath was dry. 'It's fantastic! I wish I lived here. It's perfect.'

He shrugged. 'It smells in the summer.' But he had that look that Charles got when he was secretly pleased. He said, 'Seagulls have the best feathers – look, there –' he gestured to the sheet, to the white patches – 'because they're naturally greasy, and water runs off them. But you don't get many seagulls, except after storms. Pigeon feathers aren't bad. They're thick, and I add duck grease to them, when I have it.'

'But how do you catch them?'

Matteo looked at her, very hard. 'How do you think?'

'With … with a trap?' Sophie had no idea. With a knife? With his hands? With his teeth? Nothing, she felt, would surprise her.

‘I’ll show you. I haven’t eaten today, anyway.’

Matteo reached inside the chimney and pulled out a bow. He reached under the mattress, and pulled out a bundle of arrows. ‘The arrows blow away if you don’t tie them,’ he said. ‘It gets windy up here.’ He fitted the arrow on the bow, and his face flicked into that listening expression she had seen on the tightrope. It shut her out as effectively as a door. He turned his back to Sophie. There were three pigeons roosting on the chimney stack on the rooftop they had come from; suddenly Matteo’s arm snapped back, and an arrow shrilled across the space and struck the middle pigeon in its neck. The other two pigeons took off, shrieking in fear.

‘Always aim for the middle pigeon, if there is one,’ he said. He ignored the shock in Sophie’s face. ‘It gives you more chance of hitting. And aim against the wind.’

Matteo jogged to the edge of the rooftop and crouched to peer over. Then he tipped himself forwards. Sophie watched, certain that he was going to die: but at the last minute he grasped the rope and swung, hand over hand, to the opposite rooftop. He

pulled himself up, stuffed the pigeon down the front of his shirt (So that explained the red patches, Sophie thought) and swung back over the night sky. The whole there-and-back took less than two minutes.

He dumped the bird at her feet. 'That's how I catch them,' he said, and he wiped his bloody palms in his hair. 'I never said I was nice,' he said.

Sophie tried to look unconcerned, unimpressed. 'Can I help pluck it?' she said.

'*Non.*'

'Why not? Please?'

'You can't help. You can *do* it. This isn't a dinner party.'

Luckily, Sophie had read about plucking birds. You started at the neck and worked backwards. 'I've never had pigeon,' she said. She pulled out a handful of the feathers. The bird's skin was like an old man's, and she tried not to wince. 'What does it taste like?' She tried to pluck briskly.

'Like smoky chicken,' said Matteo. 'Like heaven. But we shouldn't be talking.'

'Oh! Sorry. Will somebody hear?'

'*Non*. Not this high. But aren't you supposed to be listening for music?'

While Matteo gutted and skewered the bird, Sophie listened. What he had said was true. By standing or squatting on different parts of the rooftop, she could hear snatches of conversation and snippets of music from half a mile away.

She circled the roof in a half-crouch, listening to the sounds that came on the wind. She heard an argument, full of what must have been French swearing, and some drunken singing, and a barking dog. Mostly, though, there was just night-silence, and nightingales.

It was a shock when Matteo called, 'Sophie!'

'Yes! What is it? Do you hear something?'

'*Non*. The food's ready.'

Matteo's table manners were not the kind that win prizes. He tore at the pigeon with his back teeth, showing lots of gum, and ate with his mouth open. She tried to follow suit, but the fat on the meat was ferociously hot. The skin on the roof her mouth was flaking off.

She looked around the rooftop, and at Matteo's small piles of possessions. 'Matteo, do you have a fork?'

'No. Why?'

'Don't you need one?'

'I've got fingers, haven't I? And teeth?'

'But don't you burn yourself?'

'Never.' He held out his hands to her. 'You see? Heatproof.' The palms and fingertips were thickly calloused. 'I don't burn.'

'I'd quite like a fork,' said Sophie. 'I'm sorry. It's just, my fingers are blistering.' She needed her fingers to play the cello. 'And do you have any water?'

'For drinking, or for your fingers?'

'For both.'

'Let me see them.' He took her hand in his. 'Your hands are too soft.' Then he spat on his fingers, and rubbed them over hers.

'Keep spitting on them,' he said, 'it helps. Here. This is just for drinking.' He handed her a tin can half filled with water. 'It's rainwater. I can't waste it on burns. And don't drink it all.'

Sophie sipped. It tasted of rust, but not bad at all.

'Right,' he said. 'Stay there. I'll make you a fork.'

Matteo tore open the pigeon carcass and tugged out the wishbone and one long leg bone. 'Pass the kettle,' he said. Apparently untroubled by the boiling water, he dipped the bones in the kettle, added a tiny pinch of soot, and scrubbed.

'Soot acts as soap,' he said.

'Does it?' She looked at his face, which was black with dirt. 'Are you sure you're not thinking of … um, soap?'

'You'll see.' He kept scrubbing. 'I'm right.' And he *was* right. Soon the two bones shone white. Then he fished some string from his pocket.

'You see. String is the only thing that is never, never boring. String, and birds.'

He tied the wishbone to the top of the leg bone with a figure of eight. 'A fork!' he said. '*Voilà*.'

CHAPTER NINETEEN

Sophie slept most of the next day, and woke in her own bed to find it was raining. It rose to a storm in the night. Sophie counted the seconds between the lightning and thunder, 'One, two' – and then the boom. She did not dare go out on the rooftop. The next day was no better. Charles trudged out in an inadequate borrowed raincoat to look for lawyers.

'I'll keep lookout, if you'll let me use your window,' Sophie told him. 'Come back soon, all right? And don't get spotted.' She rubbed his sleeve, which was too short by an inch.

'I won't. And you, Sophie: make sure you don't leave

this room,' said Charles. 'Unless you absolutely have to. If you need to pee, use the chamber pot. I don't want the other guests to see you.'

So all day Sophie sat by Charles's window with a cup of cocoa in her lap, and kept lookout. She was watching for policemen, and for cello players. Almost nobody went by, and those who did were hidden by umbrellas. She strained her ears for cello music, until her head roared and she heard requiems behind every horse and cart. Every few minutes, she crossed and uncrossed her fingers.

The cup of cocoa grew a skin, and then grew cold. Sophie did not notice. The rain did not stop.

When Sophie went to bed, the rain was torrential. She woke again, though, to hear the clock striking two, and the downpour slowed to a drizzle. The clouds were

blowing across the moon, and the moonlight flashed on and off inside her room, like Morse code.

Sophie shoved back her covers, and jumped up. She felt as awake as day. She pulled on her stockings, and over them her trousers, and two jerseys. Then she cut the tips off the stockings, and rolled them back to expose her toes. She clambered out of her window, leaving it open, dripping on to the bed.

Matteo was sitting cross-legged by his fire, leaning against the largest chimney stack. He had a knife in one hand, and something pinkish in the other. It looked suspiciously like a skinned rat. Sophie whistled, and he dropped whatever it was into the embers and ran to fetch her across the tightrope.

When they reached the fire, the animal was smoking. Matteo swore.

'*Ach*. Rat is never delicious; but burned rat is disgusting.'

'What's rat like?'

Matteo sat, and pulled her down beside him. 'Sit. I didn't think you'd come, in the rain. It's like … hedgehog.'

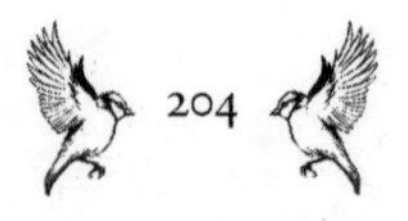

'I've never had hedgehog, either.'

'Have you eaten rabbit?' He threw a sack over her knees, and pulled one over his shoulders.

'Yes, I've had rabbit.' The sack was wet, but Sophie did not say so. His sack, she could see, was wetter.

'Well, it's not like rabbit, but it's not *not* like rabbit. Here. You can try it.'

Sophie took it, sniffed it. It did not smell inspiring.

Matteo said, 'Leave some for me, though. More than half. I'm bigger.'

'Is this breakfast?' she asked him. 'Or … dinner?'

'This is lunch. I had breakfast when I woke up. Sort of.'

'When was that?' Sophie nibbled at the rat's thigh. The rat tasted of charcoal and horse-tails. She swallowed with an effort. 'It's … not bad,' she said. 'Here, though. It's yours.'

'I don't know. Sunset. So, about nine o'clock.' Matteo tore at the rat with his teeth. 'I have supper at five o'clock in the morning. If there is any supper.'

'Why wouldn't there be?'

He shrugged. 'It's been a bad week for food.' His

face, up close, was tight-pulled and thin, and he said, 'I'm tired. Perhaps you'd better not stay long.'

'I'm so sorry!' Sophie cursed inwardly. 'I should have thought to bring food.' She had forgotten that he might be hungry. 'I didn't realise. But, Matteo, please let me stay. I need to be up here to listen.' Her skin was burning. It always did when she thought of her mother. 'Please.'

'Fine.' Matteo flopped on to his back, and stared up at the stars. 'I'm too hungry to talk, though.'

'Why is it worse than usual?'

'Why?' He half sat, and stared at her incredulously. 'The rain! The rain, obviously.'

Sophie lay down, a little way apart. In the moonlight Matteo's face was the colour of old snow. 'Does the rain make hunting harder?' she said.

'Yes. The birds go and shelter in the station. And rain makes people keep their windows shut at night. There's nothing you can pick up from window sills.'

'What've you had to eat?'

'Seagull, on Tuesday. It got blown in by the storm. It was almost dead anyway. A blue tit for breakfast.

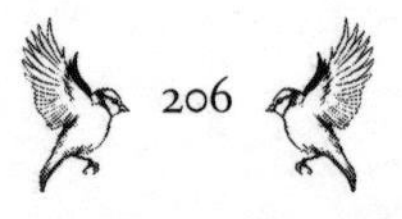

I was sorry about that. I quite like them – alive, I mean. I don't particularly like to eat them. And there's not enough meat on them to make it worth plucking them.'

Sophie couldn't help feeling awed. 'Was that all? In three days?'

'*Oui*. Or, *non* – I had a candy cane on Sunday. Anastasia and Safi left it for me in the oak tree by the Opera. I think it was meant for me. If not, it's not my problem.'

Sophie turned on to her stomach. 'Who're they? Anastasia and – what was the second name?'

His face flicked to blank. 'Nobody. Do you have any food in your pockets, maybe?'

'I don't think so.' Sophie fished in her trousers. 'No, wait – I have raisins. I was carrying them for the birds, actually, but you'd better have them.'

'Yes,' said Matteo, 'I had better. I'm hungry. Anyway, I'd just eat the birds once they'd eaten the raisins, so it's just skipping a step. What else?'

Sophie scrabbled deeper. Pockets, she thought, were why trousers were so superior to skirts.

'Yes!' She pulled out a sticky hand. 'Here – there's some chocolate. It might be quite old, though. And it melted and got mixed up with my trousers. But I think it should be all right?'

'Good. Give it to me.'

Matteo did not, as she'd expected, cram it all into his mouth. Instead he took a pan from the fire, and dropped the chocolate into it. He stirred with a whittled stick. 'Chocolate is best cooked. It makes you feel like there's more of it,' he said. He tipped the raisins into the chocolate. 'There. That smells good.'

The scent of melted chocolate was spreading over the rooftop. Matteo's body unwound a few inches. For the first time that evening, he smiled.

'See if you can bring more food, next time you come,' he said. 'It's easier, up here, when you're full.'

Charles had not had luck with the lawyers.

'It's not easy,' he said. 'None of them will take a case against the commissioner of police. Most lawyers seem to have the decency and courage of lavatory paper. But we'll find someone, my love.' They were at breakfast.

Charles spread half a jar's worth of jam on his croissant and dipped it into his coffee. 'Heaven!' he said. 'You're not eating?'

'I thought I might save it for later.' Sophie transferred the croissant to her lap, then to her pocket.

'You're not hungry?'

'No, thank you. I'm stuffed.'

Charles paused. 'Really?' His eyebrow hooked itself upwards. 'You've already hidden your bread roll in your pocket. And, if I'm not mistaken, there's an apple in your sock. What are you stuffed *with*?'

Inevitably, Sophie's thoughts collapsed in a heap. 'With biscuits,' she said.

'For breakfast? Unusual.'

'I thought I'd like to see what it was like, to have biscuits for breakfast.'

'And what was it like?'

'It was good. I had loads of them. I feel a bit sick now, actually.' She half rose. 'May I go?'

'Not just yet. Sit down, Sophie. Tell me: what sort of biscuits did you have?'

'The chocolate fudge ones.'

'The ones with the soft middle?'

'Yes.'

He smiled. 'And you didn't save me any?'

'I'm sorry. They were too delicious.'

'They certainly sound delicious. And these delicious soft-fudge chocolate biscuits: they came from where?'

'From the baker, of course.' Sophie nodded out of the window, to the baker's bright orange awning. Too late, she saw it was rolled in, and the lights were out in the windows.

'How resourceful of you.' Charles's eyebrows were bristling with irony. 'The baker doesn't open on Sundays, Sophie.'

'I know that. I bought them yesterday.'

'Nor does it open on Saturday.'

Damn, thought Sophie. Her armpits were prickling, and her face was growing sweaty. She hated lying. She wasn't sure if she was good at it; she suspected she was not. 'Oh, yes! I know, I just forgot. I meant, Friday.'

'And you paid for them with ... what? As far as I know, you have no French money.'

There was nothing to say, so Sophie said nothing.

'Is there something you'd like to tell me?'

Yes! thought Sophie. There were hundreds of things she wanted to tell him. But adults, she thought, were unpredictable, even the best ones. You never knew when they were going to stop you doing what you were doing. She tucked her fingers into her sash, and crossed them tightly.

'No,' she said. 'Nothing at all.' And then, after a pause, 'Can I go?'

'Of course.' Charles hitched his eyebrows into upside-down Vs. 'You're a very poor liar, Sophie. I do not recommend a career as an actress. But, as long as you aren't doing anything too extravagantly illegal, I am happy for you to have secrets.'

'It's nothing illegal.' Or, if it was, she thought, then it shouldn't be.

'Keep your secret, then, my darling. Everybody needs them. Secrets make you tough, and wily.' He waited another moment, but Sophie kept her gaze fixed on the rungs of his chair, and he waved her away. 'Off you go,' he said. 'Go and practise telling lies in front of a mirror.'

In a few minutes, though, he knocked on her door.

'The secret, Sophie,' he said. 'Is it a food-based secret?'

'Oh! Um, yes. Sort of.'

'Is it to do with your mother?'

'Yes. I think so.' *I hope so*, she thought. She crossed every finger and toe.

'Is another adult involved?'

'No,' said Sophie. 'No, not an adult.'

Charles seemed about to say something else. Then he shook his head. 'Good,' he said. 'Keep your secret.'

'Thank you,' said Sophie.

'But, Sophie?' Charles had turned, and she couldn't see his face.

'Yes?'

'Don't dare get hurt, or I'll skin you alive.'

That night, when Sophie went up to her room, her teeth brushed and a French dictionary under her arm, there was a pack on her bed.

The note pinned to it was in Charles's handwriting. It said, 'Everybody needs secrets. Only be sure they are

good ones.' On the back there was a P.S. 'I have never in my life had enough sausages in one sitting.'

Sophie hefted the pack. It was heavy, and squelchy in places, and something at the bottom clinked. She went to open it, and then stopped. It would be better if she and Matteo opened it together. It took a great deal of willpower not to open it until she had reached the tightrope.

There was no moon, and Matteo sat with his legs dangling over the edge of the roof, whistling.

'Look what I've got!' he called. He ran across the tightrope, jumped on to the rooftop, and took her hand. 'Come and see! Tomatoes! I've never had so many.'

The pile of tomatoes reached almost to Sophie's knee. They glistened with the dew that had fallen at sunset. She said, 'They're wonderful.' She meant it: they were just ripe, and of the large flattish variety – the sort with a swinging kick to the taste. Sophie took one and sniffed it. 'Where did you get them?' she asked.

'I grew –'

'And don't say you grew them because I won't believe you. You need a greenhouse to grow this sort.'

'Fine.' Matteo sneered, a little defiant. 'I got them from a window sill. An apartment block in the eighth arrondissement. Fifth floor.'

'So you stole them?'

'*Non*. I *took* them.'

'What's the difference?'

'If something's in the open air, that's fair game. That's hunting.'

The thought of what Miss Eliot would say to that made Sophie snort, messily. She grinned. 'What are you going to do with a hundred tomatoes?' she said.

'There's thirty-four,' he said haughtily. 'I counted.' His attention shifted from the tomatoes. 'What's in the pack?'

'I don't know. I thought we should open it together.'

'Why?'

Now that he asked, Sophie found she couldn't explain. She felt herself turning pink, and swore inwardly. 'You know. Like Christmas.'

'I don't understand. What about Christmas?'

'You know, like when you unwrap presents together at Christmas.'

'I don't,' said Matteo. His face was on edge. Perhaps he suspected her of making fun of him. He said, 'I don't know what you're talking about.'

'I think it's food,' said Sophie. 'It's from Charles.'

Food has a power over bad temper that nothing else has. Matteo's mouth elongated into a smile; it reached his ears.

'What kind of food?' He took the pack and squashed it in his hands. 'Meat?' He held it high over her head. 'Maybe I'll keep it for myself.'

'Give that back!' There was no real point in grabbing for it, but she tried anyway. He was taller than her by a head.

'We'll open it together,' he said magnanimously. He jerked it away as she came nearer. 'I'll start.'

The pack was full of parcels wrapped in greaseproof paper. Matteo dipped his face in and sniffed, then lifted out the first parcel. It was bread rolls, four of them, soft in the middle and dusted with flour at the

top. They were still warm from the oven, and they smelt of blue skies. The bread had been spread by someone with strong opinions about butter – it was as thick as the first joint of Sophie's thumb.

'I always used to think,' said Sophie, 'that if love had a smell, it would smell like hot bread.'

'What?' Matteo was eating already. 'What are you talking about?' A chunk of butter was hanging from his upper lip.

'Never mind,' said Sophie. Since Matteo looked busy, Sophie unpeeled the next package. It felt sticky in her hand.

'Meat!' said Matteo. He hadn't looked up from his two handfuls of bread roll, but he sounded gleefully certain.

'How do you know?'

'The smell.'

Matteo was right. The package unfolded away from a hunk of brown meat cut in thick slabs. It didn't look familiar. She held it out to him. 'What kind of meat is it? Can you tell?'

Matteo took the largest piece, and nibbled a corner.

'*Non*. I've never had it. It's good, though. And it's not pigeon or rat, that I do know.'

Sophie tried some. It tasted of smoke and salt. It was wonderful, up here in the night air. 'It's … venison, I think? I've never had it, but this is how I imagine it.'

Matteo's head was inside the pack. His hand came out; his fingers were wrapped around two glass bottles. 'And these? What's in these?'

'Wine, maybe?' The bottles were chilled, and perspiring in the warm air. Sophie held one against her cheek. 'They look like wine, anyway. But Charles knows I don't like wine, except champagne with blackberries.'

Matteo shrugged. 'I've never had that.' He sniffed one. Bubbles flew up his nose and he sneezed, cat-like.

Sophie laughed. 'Lemonade, I think.'

At the bottom there was half a chocolate cake, still wet and sticky in the middle, and a jam jar filled with cream, and a fat parcel wrapped in greaseproof paper and newspaper.

'Sausages!' cried Matteo. They were thick as Sophie's wrist.

Sophie counted them. 'Twenty-two,' she said. 'Eleven each.'

'*Mon Dieu!*' said Matteo. He added something else in French. Sophie didn't know the word, but it sounded unrepeatable. 'Whoever your guardian is, I love him.'

'I know! I do too.' Sophie grinned into the fire. How many other people, she thought, will give you more sausages than you have fingers and toes? 'I think we should cook them all at once,' she said. 'I think he meant us to.'

'*Non,*' said Matteo. 'We should save some for later.'

'But you don't have any ice, do you? If you don't cook them they'll spoil. I'm starving. Go on, Matteo!' A suppressed smile was twitching Matteo's left cheek. Sophie took that for a yes. 'And I could make tomato soup,' she said.

'Do you know *how* to make tomato soup?' said Matteo.

'Yes,' lied Sophie. 'At least, I'm sure I could work it out.' The sausages had no fat or gristle in them. Sophie

prodded them. 'How do we cook them? Do you have a pan?'

'No,' said Matteo, 'but I collect weathervanes.'

Sophie wondered if his English had gone awry. 'You collect … weathervanes?'

'Yes. I've got almost a dozen.' Matteo reached into a sack behind him. He pulled out a handful of long metal spikes and dropped them at Sophie's feet. Most of them were fashioned to look like arrows. One, though, was the mast of a ship, and one a chicken. The weathervanes were polished and shone bronze and silver in the moonlight.

'Here.' Matteo took three sausages, and spiked them on to the longest of the arrows. 'You do some.'

'Where do you get them?' Sophie asked.

'From rooftops, of course.'

'Isn't that stealing?' She skewered four sausages on a silver arrow, and laid them on the fire.

'No it's not. They don't use them. They let them rust. *I* use them.'

'They do use them, though. They use them to …'

'To what?'

Sophie was stymied. 'Well, to tell which way the wind is blowing, surely?'

'If they are so stupid that they need a weather-vane to tell them that, then they do not deserve weathervanes.'

'But then, nobody would have weathervanes, and there'd be none for you to steal.'

'Find, not steal.' He spat on another metal spike and rubbed it on his shirt. 'Anyway, you want to know about the wind, watch the trees! Lick your finger and feel the wind. Pull out a hair and hold it over your head.'

The sausages were starting to ooze clear juice. Within minutes the smell was quite fantastic.

Sophie rinsed Matteo's largest pot with rainwater. The pot was shaped like a small cauldron, made of brass, and it made an excellent booming sound when she tapped it with the jam jar. 'Do you have something to peel them?' she asked.

'*Non*. But you don't peel tomatoes. You're thinking of oranges.'

'I think you do if it's soup,' she said doubtfully. 'Never mind. It should be all right, shouldn't it?' She tipped

in all the tomatoes bar two. She tossed one to Matteo, and they ate them raw. 'I think we leave it to boil,' she said. As an afterthought, she tipped in half a cup of rainwater. Over the next half-hour, the tomatoes boiled down into a pulp. Their skins floated to the surface, and they fished them out – Sophie with a twig, Matteo with his fingers – and shared them with the dozen pigeons that had gathered round at the sight of crumbs.

'Can you pass the cream?' said Sophie.

'Don't use it all!' Matteo took a quick sip from the jar before he handed it to her.

'I won't.' She tipped in most of the jar, but left enough to drink with the chocolate cake. *What else would you put in soup?* she thought. She said, 'Do you have salt?'

'Of course I have salt! I'm a rooftopper, Sophie, not a savage.' Matteo kept his salt in a scrubbed-out flower-pot, twisted up in a blue square of cloth. There was pepper, too, in a red square. Sophie recognised the cloth of his shorts from the first time they met.

'I don't much like pepper,' said Sophie. 'I'll just put

in the salt, if that's all right. You can put pepper in yours.'

'Yes, you do like pepper. You just eat bad pepper in England,' said Matteo. 'I know. I've had some of the food the English leave behind. Add just a little.' He took the pepper from her, and cracked it between two scraps of slate, and tipped it in. 'Trust me.'

Sophie added the salt to the soup. The smell was so rich it made her nose shiver.

'It's ready, I think,' she said.

They sat side by side, with their backs to the wind, and drank the soup out of tin cans. The taste made her giddy. It made her want to laugh. Matteo ate whole sausages in a single mouthful. Sophie took four and made them into sandwiches with the venison. She added a slop of soup as a relish, and they ate them with both hands. Sophie's hair blew in her mouth, and she tied it back with one of Matteo's bowstrings. She couldn't remember having been so happy before.

They had made their way through fourteen of the sausages and even Matteo was slowing, when Sophie froze.

'Can you hear that?'

''ear wha'?' Matteo spoke with his mouth full. 'It's jusht the wind.'

'That's not the wind.' It was too sharp and too sweet to be the wind. 'It's music. It's a cello. Hear the low notes?' Sophie dropped her food on the slate. She strained her ears. A tune came to her over the rooftops.

She said, 'It's Fauré's *Requiem* played double time.'

Sophie leaped up, spilling sausages into the fire. 'It's coming from over there!' She tore to the far edge of the rooftop and stood on the tips of her toes on the very edge of the roof, straining to hear. *My mother*, she thought. *I am hearing my mother*. The thought shook her to her bones.

'Can you hear it?' She held her breath to listen. The music had stopped. 'God, Matteo, please! Say you heard it!'

Matteo stood and wiped his mouth. 'I heard it.'

'How far away do you think it was? Can we go now? Come on! We'll go right now! Which way's fastest?'

'I don't know.'

'What? Yes you do! You said you knew the whole of Paris! We need to go, now!'

'No.'

'What are you … look, quick, come on! Come *on*!'

'We can't just run.'

'Yes, we *can*!'

'Stop, Sophie! Listen – it's stopped, anyway.' He was white. 'It could be miles away. You can't be sure where it came from. Didn't you know? Sound twists on rooftops. It echoes. It bluffs.'

'But I could tell! It was coming from there!' Sophie pointed across the city. 'There! The Gare du Nord! The train station!'

Matteo didn't look at her. 'I know,' he said.

'Then why did you just say you didn't? Let's *go*.'

'I don't go to the station. You can go, if you like. I can't.'

'Yes, you can! I need you! You have to!'

'I can't. The rooftops there belong to someone else.'

'To who?'

He shook his head. 'I can't explain.'

'Well, in that case can we *go*?' Her heart was booming in her ears. She had heard her mother play.

'We can go. But not tonight. If you want to go to the station, we'll need the others.'

'The others?' This was annoyingly cryptic. Sophie said, 'Who? The other who?'

Matteo sighed. 'The other rooftoppers.'

'But you said there weren't any others.'

'I know. I lied.' Then he turned to her. His gaze was the sort that sees your soul, and makes you wonder where to put your hands. 'You said you could swim, didn't you?' he said.

CHAPTER TWENTY

Two days later Sophie sat on a bench in the Tuileries Garden, fidgeting with her clothes. Her heart was hummingbirding. Matteo had sent her to sit there, in the dusk, and wait.

'I sent word,' he had said. 'I signalled. They might come. They might not.'

'Who is "they"?' Sophie had watched him scrubbing the mud off snails in a pan of water. He didn't look up at her as he spoke. She had felt herself growing increasingly tight around the chest. 'And how long do I wait?'

'Maybe four hours, starting at dusk.'

'Four *hours*?'

'Or, five, to make sure.'

'Five!'

'Waiting is a talent. You have to learn it.' Matteo laid each snail he cleaned upside down in front of the fire. He had a row of them; Sophie counted eleven. Their shells were mottled, and more beautiful than she had realised. Matteo said, 'It's like playing the cello.'

'No, it's not.'

'It will be good for you.'

'What do I tell Charles? I'm not allowed on the streets. I'll get caught.' Just the word, caught, made Sophie turn cold.

'Anything. Nothing. Whatever you want. Lie to him. It doesn't matter. It will be dark.' It did matter, Sophie

thought, hugely. But Matteo was a rooftopper, and he had never known what it is like to have to lie to the person who loves you most.

Sophie resolved to say nothing to Charles; it would be better, at any rate, than lying. And she could wear a scarf round her hair. She thought, *It's my hair that they're looking out for.* And she could perhaps pad out her clothes to make herself look fatter; or slouch, to make herself look short. All the same, the thought made her ache with fear.

She said, 'Couldn't you come and keep me company?'

From the look Matteo gave her, she might have asked him to eat an unplucked pigeon. 'I don't go on the streets. Ever.'

'Then, couldn't we meet on my rooftop? Or yours? Otherwise I might get lost,' she said. 'Or caught. Please, Matteo. The police here look cruel.'

'*Non*. They don't like roofs much. They like open spaces.'

'What do you mean? You said they were rooftoppers.'

'They are, sort of.'

'Why won't you just *explain*?'

Matteo shrugged, and threw the snails into a pot of boiling broth. 'You can never know who will tell. Often the ones who look safest are worst.'

'You think I'm going to tell?'

Matteo made a face. 'It will be fine. You'll see.'

She had been sitting there for an hour. It hadn't been easy to get out. She had waited in her room for dusk, climbed out on to the rooftop and shinned down the drainpipe.

She had left a note under Charles's door:

Gone to bed early. Don't wake me. Love, S.

The thought of him finding her gone was gnawing at her insides. And every time a man in uniform passed, she jumped, and bit slithers off the inside of her mouth.

Sophie looked about for something to keep her mind off policemen. The park was emptying as it grew dark, and there wasn't much to see; only flowerbeds, which are boring unless you are allowed to pick the

flowers, and sparrows, and beside her on the bench a cheese roll for her dinner. She broke off a corner, and tossed it at the sparrows. Behind her, a voice spoke.

'That won't work. Those sparrows only eat croissant.'

Sophie whipped round.

A girl was sitting on the back of the bench with her feet on the seat. Her blonde hair was inches from Sophie's face, but Sophie hadn't heard a rustle; not a click, not a pigeon's whisper.

'You – how did you do that? That's incredible.'

The girl grinned. 'Good evening to you too. You must be Sophie.' She slid down to sit next to Sophie. 'The birds are very spoilt around here. There's a dove that only eats pain au chocolat.' She took the bread from Sophie, and, instead of throwing it to the pigeons, she bit into it. 'Oh, yum. Oh heaven. I haven't had bread for weeks.'

'It's stale.' Sophie couldn't think of anything better to say.

The girl shrugged. She licked the bread to moisten it. 'Stale means old, doesn't it? Old is wise. Wise bread. This is Safi, my sister. Say *bonsoir*, Safi.'

Sophie jumped half an inch. A dark-haired girl was lolling against the bench. The girl said nothing.

Sophie said, 'But I didn't hear you! How did you do that?'

The first girl shrugged. 'Practice.'

The dark girl came and sat on the bench, tight-rolled, almost in her sister's lap. A clock chimed, and a man began to light the street lamps. For the first time, Sophie could see them clearly.

Both were small, and filthy. The blonde wore a cotton dress; it was greenish-brown but, judging by the stitching, Sophie guessed it had once been white. It looked as if someone had deliberately smeared it with grass stains. A beetle was clinging to the hem. Somehow, the girl made it look like the richest Chinese silk.

'I'm Anastasia,' she said. Her accent was odd, Sophie thought; it was French, but there was an odd twang to the vowels. The girl spread out her arms, as though she owned the place. 'Welcome to Paris.'

'Thank you. I'm Sophie.'

'Yes. We established that,' said Anastasia. She laid her hand on the arm of her sister. 'Safi says welcome,

also.' The dark-haired girl had the face of someone who had seen a lot, and wouldn't mind punching most of it. She wore a boy's shirt and a man's pair of trousers, held up at the waist with measuring tape tied in a knot. She had something sticky smeared up one cheek, which might or might not have been blood; but beneath it, she was as beautiful as the blonde. Sophie winced with jealousy.

The blonde girl smiled. 'Matteo said you would be easy to spot. Look out for eyes the colour of candle-light, he said.'

'Matteo told you?'

'Of course. Who else?'

Sophie narrowed her eyes. '*How* did he tell you?'

'We signal. With candles. You know. Morse code, you call it? Shush, just for a second.' She looked Sophie up and down, and then jumped up and circled her to view her from the back, all without any apparent worry of being rude. Sophie tried to keep her face blank.

The girl said, 'You're very like he said. He talked about you quite a lot.'

The other girl raised her eyebrows, and said more nothing.

Unaccountably, Sophie blushed. 'What did he say about me?'

The girl shook her head. 'That's a secret.'

Sophie scowled. She felt stupid, and she looked angrily at the floor.

Anastasia said, 'It was all interesting, and mostly good.' The other girl nodded, and became more emphatically silent. Sophie tried to smile.

Anastasia said, 'Safi wanted you to know that she's very excited about meeting you.'

Safi was hiding it well, Sophie thought. But she only said, 'Why?'

'Matteo doesn't usually like people. So when he does, it matters.'

Sophie burned. She ducked behind her hair, and tried to think of something to say. 'Can I ask you something? You're French, aren't you?'

'Of course,' said Anastasia, and Safi thumped her chest. Anastasia said, '*Vive la France!*'

'Then, who taught you to speak English?'

'The American tourists.'

'Really?' Sophie hadn't expected that. 'Oh. That was nice of them.'

'They don't know they're doing it, but they eat in the cafés in the park and sit on the benches and chat chat chat.'

'And you sit on benches near them?'

'*Non!* Of course not! The park rangers would start to recognise us. We sit in the trees. They never see us. Americans are not good at seeing things.'

'Aren't they?' Sophie had never met an American.

'The adults aren't, anyway. The children are quick-eyed. You've got to be careful of the children. We speak Russian, too, and either Italian or Spanish. We're not sure which it is, but we speak it. Matteo speaks German, but not as well as he pretends he can.'

'And you're sisters?'

'Yes. Safi is younger, I think,' said Anastasia. 'At least, I think I can remember her not being around, but she can't remember the world without me. So.'

This seemed extraordinary to Sophie. She said,

'You *think* Safi is younger? Don't you know how old you are?'

Anastasia shrugged. '*Non.* We don't remember having a mother. Neither does Matteo. He keeps saying he is fourteen, but he forgets it has to go up every year.' Anastasia looked Sophie up and down again. There was a straightforwardness in her look Sophie had never seen in the girls at home. She seemed fearless. 'How old are you? We're about the same height, aren't we?'

Sophie shook her head. 'You can't tell that way. I'm tall for my age. You look about thirteen, to me.'

'Good. I will be thirteen. Safi can be ... what do you think?'

'Eleven? Ten, maybe?'

'Let's say ten,' said Anastasia. 'I like to be older.' She smoothed down her dress, like a princess at a birthday party, rather than someone with algae caked in her nails. 'Please excuse my dress. It was white brocade, once. It was so good, I found it in a dustbin. People throw away so much in Paris. But, you can't wear

white, if you want to stay safe. So we stain everything, with … *ach*, what's the word?'

'With paint? With grass?'

'There's a green dust you get coating the trees. Like tree powder, you know?'

'Yes! I know what you mean! You can find it in white, too, actually, on willow trees. Charles – my guardian – calls it wild paint. I don't know what it's really called.' Sophie looked down at her own, cream-coloured jersey. 'Will this be all right?'

'The trousers, yes. The top …' The girl shrugged. 'No, not really. White, and yellow – those are the most visible colours at night. And cream, and pink. They are like wearing a sign, "look at me". They're for people who want to be at the centre of attention.'

Sophie did not agree. Her cream jersey was very plain, and she had knitted it herself, in thick and uneven stitches. It had never occurred to her that it might be attention-seeking. She crossed her arms defensively across her chest.

Anastasia laughed. 'It's a very good jumper. You mustn't be offended. But if you don't want to be

caught, you can't ever allow people to look too much at you – you see?' Her English seemed to be faltering. 'In exchange, we have the sky. *Tu comprends, oui?* You understand?'

Sophie nodded doubtfully. 'Yes. Or, sort of.' Anastasia watched her with steady eyes. 'Not really.' Sophie grinned. 'I don't see how you can *have* the sky.'

'More than anyone else, the sky belongs to us.' It was what Matteo had said about the rooftops.

Sophie said, 'How? In what way?'

Safi tapped Sophie on the elbow. She rubbed her arms, and pointed at the clouds.

Anastasia smiled. 'She says, because we live nearer the sky than anyone else. She says, look up.'

Sophie's eyes followed the girl's pointing finger. Amongst the uppermost leaves of the tallest tree in the park, which towered above all surrounding buildings, there were strung two hammocks. They were greyish-brown, and – Sophie shaded her eyes against the setting sun – it looked as though they might be made out of sacking. She would never have spotted them, if she hadn't been shown where to look.

'They are made from the sails of a ship which washed up down the river,' said Anastasia. 'Before that we used curtains from a theatre that burned down, but the sails are better. The canvas is very strong, especially if you sew it double-thick. We dyed them with squid ink.' Anastasia's face was lit with pride. She might have been showing Sophie a country estate. 'We use sacks for blankets. You only need six or seven to keep properly warm. In the summer, we don't use them, and we hide them on the rooftop of the opera house so they don't get stolen.'

'Who would steal a sack?'

Anastasia looked shocked. 'Hundreds of people. I would. Sacks are valuable.'

The hammocks rocked very slightly in the breeze. They looked wonderfully comfortable. Sophie's heart screwed tight with envy.

Anastasia said, 'You see, Matteo, he is a rooftop boy. But, we are better with trees than buildings. We're called *arbroisiers* – tree-dwellers. And there are some boys who live in railway-station roofs: railway is *gare* in French, so we say, *gariers*.' She screwed up her face.

'The *gariers* are … *pas bien*, you know? Bad. They steal, they cheat, they cut.'

'Cut what?'

'People. Each other, sometimes. Matteo, once. But they are still sky-treaders.'

'Still what?'

'Is that not English? Um … *danseurs du ciel*. Sky-steppers. It's what we call the children who live outside, but not homeless. Not on the streets; those are just street children. They're no good. Streets can never be a home, because other people use them, all the time, and your home must be private. The trees are our home, Safi and me. Sky-treaders, you see?'

'Why do you do it, though? I mean, your hammocks look lovely – but don't you get wet? And hungry? And how do you wash? And … the toilet? It must be difficult.'

Anastasia's gaze shifted from Sophie's eyes to the space above her head. The shutters of her face came down. 'We prefer it. Nobody can lock you in a tree.'

Sophie was not stupid. She changed the subject. 'So – should I stain my jersey, before we go?'

Safi glanced up at the sun, and then shook her head. She motioned to her chest, and Anastasia nodded.

'Safi says no. She says, there isn't really time. If you want to come with us, you can wear her spare jumper. She stores it in the oak next to the statue of Napoleon.'

'That oak?' It was a great pillar of a tree, the first six feet wide as a giant. 'She can climb that one?'

'Yes. We both can. I have a scarf and gloves in a hole in the cedar tree. We spread our things out; all the sky-steppers do. That way, if one thing gets taken, you've got more.' She looked again at Sophie's jersey. 'Safi's jumper is grey. Grey will be better. Where we're going is very grey.'

'Thank you,' said Sophie. She looked doubtfully at the smear on Safi's cheek. 'Are you sure? I mean – it's very kind of you.'

'Safi will go and get it now.' The girls seemed to be waiting. Anastasia said, 'You have to give her your jersey, in exchange.'

'Oh!' Sophie flushed, deeply, and began to pull it off. 'Of course, yes,' she said, her voice muffled by the wool. 'Sorry.'

As Safi ran off with the jumper bundled in her arms, Sophie gathered the courage to ask a question. 'Doesn't she talk?'

'Of course, sometimes. But not when other people are around.'

Sophie tried to look like she understood. 'Was she always like that?'

Anastasia looked as though she were deciding whether or not to be insulted. Then she said, 'We – sky-treaders – we're different. I guess you become strange, even if you didn't start out strange.'

That made sense to Sophie. It was something she'd thought about before. 'I think, actually, everyone starts out with some strange in them. It's just, whether or not you decide to keep it.'

'Maybe. Yes. I could believe that.'

They watched Safi glance around, then launch herself at the oak. There were no low branches, but she gripped with her knees and dug with her nails. In ten seconds she had disappeared amongst the foliage.

Sophie's head was swirling with these new revelations. 'How did she do that?'

'Practice,' said Anastasia.

The sun had almost set. Sophie wrapped her arms around her knees and shivered. Sunset seemed a good moment to ask questions. Sophie said, 'Anastasia? Why do I need a grey jersey? Where are we going?'

'Matteo didn't tell you?'

'No. He doesn't tell me much. And he's hard to guess.'

'Ah, I know! Safi is too. Likes cats, *non*? We're going to visit someone. A fighter. To go to the station, we need numbers, you see?'

'And do they … does this person live in the river?'

'Why?'

'Matteo asked if I could swim.'

'Ah! The person we're going to see can't swim, and he always wants money.'

'Where will we get the money? Why does it matter he can't swim?'

'You'll see. I think Matteo didn't want me to tell.'

'Doesn't he beg, this person who wants money? I've seen street children doing it.'

'Of course not!' Anastasia glared and moved a few

inches down the bench. 'I told you, we're not street children. Begging would be boring and stupid and dangerous. We buy food, like normal people. Only, mostly from stalls, at night, because –' She held up her hands. They were layered thick with calluses. 'My hands make me memorable, you see? It's dangerous to be memorable. But I need them like that for climbing; it's like having gloves. And Safi won't go near stall owners.'

'Why not? What's wrong with stall owners?'

'*Rien*. I mean, nothing.' Anastasia shrugged. 'Safi's like Matteo. She does not want too much human in her life. She'd like it better if it was just her and me.'

Sophie knew that feeling. But before she had time to reply, someone tapped her on the shoulder. Safi stood behind her, clasping a grey rag to her chest.

'Don't *do* that!' cried Sophie. 'I swallowed my tongue.'

Anastasia laughed. Even Safi twitched around the lips.

'Let's go,' said Anastasia. 'Matteo will meet us there, half an hour after dark. It should be dark by the time we get there.'

'Where are we going?'

'It's not far. The Pont de Sainte Barbara. It's a bridge.' She took Sophie's hand. 'You'll like it. It's beautiful; it's like you, actually.'

CHAPTER TWENTY-ONE

The bridge was indeed beautiful, though it wasn't much like Sophie; at least, Sophie couldn't see it. It was fine wrought, with gold-painted railings and pigeons roosting on each end.

They ran, the three of them, down stone steps and came to rest under the bridge. Matteo wasn't anywhere.

'Did he say he'd be waiting?' said Sophie. 'Can you see him?'

'He'll be here somewhere,' said Anastasia. She whistled, not very well, the same whistle Matteo had used

on the tightrope. They waited. Matteo was still nowhere.

'You try,' said Anastasia. 'He said you had a good whistle.'

Sophie tried to remember the shape her lips had made. She whistled; and then again, louder, and sharper.

'Again,' said Anastasia.

Sophie whistled until her lips buzzed and her ears hurt. She was just about to give up when there was a thump, and Matteo appeared, walking swiftly along the railing of the bridge.

'*Bonsoir!*' He sat on the rail, and called down to them. 'Are you ready?'

'Ready for what? Why won't you tell me?' Sophie hissed. 'And keep your voice down. I can't be seen.'

'I thought you might not come if I told you. Take off your shoes.'

'Why wouldn't I come?' Sophie bent to untie her laces.

'Because the water's so cold,' he said, matter-of-factly. 'It's like swimming in frostbite. We're going river-sieving.'

'River-sieving?' Sophie halted, one shoe in her hand.

'Diving for coins. If I really need money, I collect coins, from under the bridges. And sometimes there's wedding rings. People throw them in. I don't know why –' He shrugged. 'But you can sell them, sometimes.'

'But those coins are wishes! You're stealing other people's wishes!'

The look Matteo gave her was so flinty she could have chipped a tooth on it. 'If you have money to waste on wishes, you don't need the wishes as badly as I need the money.' He stood on the rail, rose on to his toes, and disappeared in a flawless dive.

Sophie stood at the edge, waiting. It was almost two

minutes before his head came up. He swam to the edge and dropped a handful of coppers at her feet.

'You said you could swim?' he said. 'Safi and Stasia can't, much.'

'I can, yes. I might not have told you if I'd known why you were asking.' Sophie crouched at the water's edge. It was midnight blue, and the stars shone on its surface. It looked secretive. Sophie bent until she could see her reflection. She looked secretive, too, and more beautiful than she had expected. She dipped a finger in the water. 'My God, Matteo!' It was icy. Her toes contracted in protest.

'Then come on,' said Matteo. 'There's a lot. If we leave it there, the *gariers* will take it.' And, as Sophie ran to the edge, he hissed, 'Take your other shoe off, first! And quietly.'

'I was going to!' She pulled off her shoe and trousers and jersey and bundled them into a corner under the bridge, but left her pants and vest. She glared at him, and dived – with some splash, but still quite well, she thought – into the water.

'Ugh. It's freezing!' Sophie gasped and retched as the water clutched at her. She spat out a mouthful.

'You sound like a water buffalo,' said Matteo, treading water. 'Come this way. The tides shift most of the coins to the left – over here. Keep moving, or your heart stops.'

He dived under and she waited, kicking her frozen feet, until he came up.

'Matteo!' she said. 'Listen to me. I won't help until you tell me something.'

'What? I'm icing over inside, Sophie. This isn't a good moment.'

'Those boys who live on the station. What's wrong with them?'

Matteo shrugged, which is not easy to do while treading water. He said, 'They're dirty.'

Sophie said nothing. She tried not to let her gaze flick to the girls standing on the bank, dressed in mud and rags.

Matteo saw. Matteo, Sophie thought, saw everything. It was very annoying. 'There's good dirt and bad dirt,' he said to her. 'The *gariers* are bad dirt.'

'Which is which, though?' said Sophie. 'What counts as good dirt?'

'Je ne sais pas.' Matteo scowled at her, as he always did when she asked questions. 'I don't know. *Ach, je m'en fous.'*

'He says, he doesn't know, he doesn't care,' called Anastasia. She must have been listening from the bank of the river. 'I suppose, good dirt is soil. And roofdust.' Safi made a sign. Anastasia added, 'And treedust, also.'

Matteo said, 'And the grit you get if you run your hand along the top of a stone bridge. Bad dirt is dried blood.'

'And sewerage. And the chimneydust on bad days.'

Sophie knew that by now. The chimney smoke could be corrosive in the nostrils.

'Usually it's not too bad,' said Anastasia, 'but when there's no wind and the air is damp, it sucks up the smoke and wipes it over your face.' Sophie had noticed. She had also noticed that Matteo picked his nose a lot more than most people; and that on smoggy days the snot was black.

'And pigeon fat,' said Anastasia. 'Pigeon fat's bad dirt.'

'*Non!*' said Matteo. He turned and swam away from them. 'No, pigeon fat's good dirt.'

Anastasia exchanged a meaningful look with Sophie. 'A tiny bit is OK, maybe. More than a tiny bit and you start smelling like an open wound. Anyway, it's not just dirt. They're vicious, the *gariers*. They're like animals.'

Sophie thought about that. Matteo had always struck her as being like an animal: a cat, or a fox. Anastasia and Safi moved with the same shifts and swing as monkeys. 'Is that bad? To be like animals?'

Anastasia said, 'They're like dogs. Have you ever seen a mad dog? They're cruel in the eyes.'

'Do they … bite?' She had expected the two girls to laugh, but they just stared back at her. Nobody moved, or smiled.

At last, Safi nodded. Matteo popped up next to her, panting. He said, 'Yes. They bite. Come on. Before my teeth freeze together.'

There was very little current, so the swimming was

easy, but the water was murky and in the dark it was almost impossible to see the glint of copper. Sophie found what she could by groping about the riverbed. She and Matteo dived six, then seven times, swimming to the side whenever they had a handful. She was gratified to find that her pile on the bank was double the size of his.

'*Ach!* It's my fingers,' he said. Sophie and Anastasia exchanged another glance. 'I can't feel what's a coin and what's a stone.'

'Of course,' said Sophie. 'Of course it is.'

When Anastasia called out that they had more than three francs, Matteo said that was enough. They swam, half racing, to the bank. Sophie was faster, but Matteo reached out and ducked her under just as she was reaching out for the edge.

'Cheat!' She came up spitting. 'You're a filthy cheater.'

'Cheating doesn't exist for rooftoppers,' said Matteo. 'There's just alive, or dead.'

'Anyway, that's not cheating,' said Anastasia. 'That's fighting. Fighting's better than cheating.' She hauled

Sophie out of the water, and handed her a square of chocolate.

Matteo stayed in the water. Anastasia passed him another square, and he ate it treading water.

'Thank you,' said Sophie. Her voice came out in a croak. 'Swimming always makes me thirsty. Can I drink the river water?'

'No! Sorry. Rat disease. Even Matteo doesn't, and he's immune to most things. There'll be water when we get to the cathedral, though,' said Anastasia.

'The cathedral?' Sophie pulled on her borrowed jersey, and stuffed wet feet into her shoes. 'What cathedral?'

'*The* cathedral, of course. Matteo'll meet us there.'

'Meet us there? But he's here –' Sophie's head whipped round. Matteo had gone.

'He's like that,' said Anastasia. 'He'll be going by the river, and then the trees.'

Safi approached her silently, and stroked down the parts of Sophie's hair that were scarecrowing, and picked out the pondweed. She took Sophie's scarf from the ground, and wound it round Sophie's head.

'Oh!' said Sophie. 'I almost forgot about my hair!' Her whole body swept with terror, and she tugged at the cloth, far down over her ears. 'That was so stupid of me. Thank you.' Safi smiled; and then she suddenly blushed purple. She darted up the stairs and into the leaves of one of the trees lining the pavement.

'Will she be all right?' said Sophie.

Anastasia gathered up the coins and stowed them in her pockets. 'Of course. She'll go by treetop too,' she said. '*Allez*. If we walk quickly you'll be dry by the time we reach Notre Dame. Race you up the stairs.'

CHAPTER TWENTY-TWO

Dark pavements are one of the best places in the world to talk. They walked quickly, so Sophie wouldn't get cold. Anastasia hummed under her breath. Sophie waited until she was sure Matteo was nowhere close before she spoke.

'Anastasia? If I ask you something, could you not tell Matteo I asked?'

'Maybe. Probably. I'll try, anyway. What is it?'

'It's the … is it, *gariers*? The train station boys. Why does Matteo hate them? He goes blank when he talks about them.'

'Oh. If you don't know, I don't know if I should tell you.'

'Please. It frightens me. His face goes dark.'

Anastasia ran her nails over iron railings as they passed. Under her touch, they played music. 'There was a fight. A few years ago. The *gariers*, they didn't want anyone else on the rooftops. Safi and I, we didn't care much. We moved to the trees. Trees are better. But Matteo, he loves being a rooftopper. Rooftops are ...' She stopped, and made a face. '*Ach*, this will sound too poetic.'

'Say it anyway.'

'They are all he has,' said Anastasia. She flushed. 'Sorry. *Alors*, he couldn't give them up.'

'What happened?'

'Nobody won. They bit …'

'Bit what?' Sophie stared at the girl, who looked away. 'Bit *what*?'

'Nothing. Matteo lost the tip of his finger. A *garier* lost his hand. And, have you seen Matteo's stomach? The scar?'

'He said he fell on a weathervane!'

'Did he? Well, he lied. He almost died. He had to go to an orphanage for medicine. You know about that, *oui*? And now he never goes near the station, and never goes on the ground.' Anastasia halted, and grasped Sophie's arm.

'Stop. We're nearly there. Matteo will be somewhere around.' Her face was restless in the starlight. She bit her lip. 'Promise you won't tell him I told you?'

'Of course,' said Sophie, but the buildings around them were distracting. They stood at the foot of a great white building. It rose up into the night sky, majestic as a god. 'What is this? Where are we?'

'Notre Dame, of course! And Matteo's in that tree, you see? By the door.' Sophie couldn't see; but Safi was

standing underneath it, looking up at the leaves. The courtyard was empty. Anastasia said, 'Let's go.'

Notre Dame was as painful to climb as it was beautiful to look at. The scramble to the top took twice as long as Sophie had expected.

Matteo went first, followed by Safi. They seemed to know it as well as Sophie knew her home in London; their hands found grips and holds in the stone without a second's hesitation. Sophie followed more slowly. Anastasia came last, giving advice on handholds and guiding Sophie's feet when she got stuck.

Balancing came more easily to Sophie now. Her feet were still tender against the stone, and her toes bled a little, but she was determined not to wince in front of the rooftoppers. They were not, she thought, the wincing sort. She rubbed her foot with spit, bit the inside of her cheek. By the time she was halfway up it was pulpy with chewing. Twice she lost her footing, but she did not think anyone noticed.

To most things in life, there is no trick; but to

balance, Sophie thought, there was a trick of sorts. The trick was knowing where to find your centre; balance lay somewhere between her stomach and her kidneys. It felt like a lump of gold in amongst brown organs. It was difficult to find, but once found, it was like a place marked in a book; easy to recover. Balance is also to do with thinking. Sophie tried to think of mothers, and music; and not of dropping backwards on to the pavement below.

Paris lay still below them. From where Sophie stood, with both her hands wrapped round the neck of a carved saint, it was a mass of silver, except where the river shone a rusty-gold colour in the lamplight. 'It's beautiful,' Sophie said. 'I didn't realise the river was so beautiful!'

'Yes.' Anastasia looked taken aback. 'It's … brown, mostly.'

When they reached the base of the tower, Matteo and Safi were perched close together, scratching noughts and crosses into the slate with a nail. From their faces, they might have just sauntered up a flight of stairs.

'A tie,' said Matteo. He scratched out the game. 'Sophie, can you whistle? We need to call Gérard.'

'Yes, of course.' The three waited. She felt suddenly self-conscious. 'Um. The tune you use on the birds?'

'Yes. Make it loud; as loud as you can. He might be asleep.'

Sophie whistled the three notes she had heard on the tightrope. There was a pause; then the three notes came back, deeper and richer than she'd sent them.

'Was that an echo?'

'*Non.*' Matteo cupped his hands, and gave two owl hoots. 'That was Gérard.'

Up above them, from the bell tower, there was a small avalanche of dust, and a boy appeared. He swung down hand over hand, finding footholds on the open jaws of the gargoyles. He somersaulted down the last four feet, and landed facing Sophie.

'*Bonsoir,*' he said.

His face was younger than Matteo's, but his legs were so long that he towered above them both. He was so thin that Sophie could have snapped him, she thought, with one hand. He did not look like a fighter.

'*Salut*, Gérard,' said Matteo. 'We want to borrow you.'

The boy grinned. '*Bon*. I know. Anastasia signalled.' He wore a musty, weevil-eaten jacket, which looked as though he had made it himself from a selection of doormats. Sophie coveted it immediately.

'Hello,' she said. 'I'm Sophie.'

'*Oui*,' he said. 'I know.' His English was a little halting, but he had a good face. His eyebrows were thick enough to shine shoes with, and his eyes were gentle. 'You need to go to the station, yes?' He hesitated. He was obviously too polite, Sophie thought, to be good at life. He said, 'Did you … bring me anything?'

'Yes,' said Anastasia. 'Of course.' She tipped the still-wet coins into his cupped hands.

'*Merci!* Did you know, the candles in the cathedral, they have gone up to twenty centimes? *C'est fou!*'

Sophie said, 'Couldn't you just … take some? If you needed them? I'm sure they wouldn't mind.'

'*Non!* You can't steal from the church! That's a sin.'

'What do you do for light, then? When you can't get candles?'

'Mostly, nothing. Your eyes get better at dark. Dark is a talent. Or, you can put oil-soaked cloths in tin cans and light them.'

'If you have cloths,' said Anastasia.

'If you have oil,' said Matteo.

Gérard laughed, an inward, guilty laugh. 'So. We go to the station, yes? To fight, *oui*?'

'Perhaps to fight,' said Anastasia. 'Hopefully just to listen.' She turned to Sophie. 'Gérard is good at listening.'

Matteo did not seem jealous. He nodded. 'It's true. Listening is unusual. Animals have it. Most people only think they do.'

Gérard said, 'I can hear a harmonica played in a classroom halfway down the river.'

'That's impossible!' said Sophie. 'Isn't it?'

'Not impossible,' said Gérard. 'Just unusual.'

It wasn't polite to whisper, but she had to. She pulled Anastasia to one side, and cupped her hands round the girl's ear. 'Is he telling the truth?' she breathed. 'Is he just boasting? It's *so* important. Does he realise how important it is?'

Gérard laughed. It was hard to tell in the dark, but he seemed to be blushing. 'Yes, he is,' he said, 'and yes, he does. Whispering doesn't work around me. I didn't ask to be born like this – it makes sleeping difficult. I have to wear acorns in my ears. But it is true. I think it comes from living on a church.'

Anastasia said, 'He sings, too. He practises the choir's songs every night, when they've left.'

Matteo scowled. 'I *said* he sings. Didn't I, Sophie?'

Anastasia rolled her eyes. '*Boys*. He doesn't just sing. With him, it's like the first snow. Sing something, Gérard.'

Gérard wrinkled his nose. '*Non*.'

Safi tapped her chest, and held out her hand towards him. She tilted her head.

'Please, Gérard?' said Sophie. 'One song. For luck.'

'*Ach, d'accord*,' said Gérard. 'Fine. *Half* a song.' He glanced around, and licked a finger to check which way the wind was blowing. He cleared his throat.

The first notes from Gérard's mouth were so clear and sweet that they sent tingles from Sophie's scalp all the way down to her toes. The words were in French,

but it certainly wasn't a hymn. It made you want to bunch up your skirts and dance with the people you love. It made Sophie want to twirl. It made her want her mother so much it hurt.

There was silence when Gérard stopped. Even the river was hushed.

Then Sophie and Anastasia burst into cheers. They clapped, and stamped against the cathedral roof. Safi made a shrill whooping in the back of her throat. It was the first noise Sophie had heard her make.

A throat was cleared. 'If you hadn't been making enough noise to wake the saints,' said Matteo, 'you would have heard the clock strike midnight. We should get a move on, if we want to be at the station at two.'

'Why two?' said Gérard. 'Two is a bad hour for *gariers*. We should go later.'

'Two was when Sophie heard the music last.' Matteo gave a grunt. 'I know it's not much to go on,' he said, 'but I thought it would be better than nothing.'

'It's a possible,' said Sophie. She said it quietly, so the others wouldn't hear. 'You should never ignore a possible.'

CHAPTER TWENTY-THREE

They reached the neighbourhood of the station just before two o'clock in the morning. The rooftops had grown steadily lower as they had moved away from Notre Dame, and the others were on edge and anxious.

Twice, they had to cross a road between buildings. Matteo, Gérard and Safi jumped from a cedar tree to a lamp post and swung effortlessly to the drainpipe on the far side. Anastasia and Sophie slid down one drain-pipe, ran across the road, and grasped the next pipe. It had handholds at regular intervals, but there is

nothing like climbing a drainpipe at night to remind you just how dark dark can be.

The five came to rest on the roof of a school. The four rooftoppers sat, alert, in a square, facing outwards. Sophie sat a little to one side. She held her breath, and prayed. She whispered to herself, 'Please. Please let me find her.' Her heart was thumping hard enough to break, but the words sounded too small and thin in the night air. Sophie clenched her fists, and sat on them.

An hour passed. Sophie grew restless. None of the rooftoppers had spoken. They had not moved a muscle.

At last she whispered, 'Can I ask you all a question?'

Matteo grunted. Gérard said, 'Of course you can. What?'

'What happens when rooftoppers grow up?'

'Oh!' said Matteo. 'I thought you were going to ask about toilets.'

Gérard said, 'Mostly, they go down to the ground, but they still lead wildish sort of lives. It is easier to be a wildish sort of adult than a child.'

Anastasia sniffed, haughty as a Cleopatra. 'Especially,' she said, 'if you happen to be a boy.'

'And have there been others?' said Sophie. 'In the past?'

Anastasia said, 'No', just as Matteo said, 'Yes.'

'Yes,' he said again. 'I think so. Look. I found this on my roof, when I first moved there.' Matteo took from his pocket a small knife. It was ornate and heavy. 'See the handle?' It looked at least a hundred years old. On the handle, finger grooves were clearly visible. The hand that had made them was smaller than Sophie's.

'Whose was it?' she asked.

'Some kid.' He shrugged. 'A clever kid. I found it wrapped in rope. Rope is the best way to store a knife. Not everyone knows that.'

'Did you ever go looking for them?' Sophie thought she would have, if it had been her. 'Why didn't they come back for it?'

'*Non*. It was rusted a centimetre thick. It must have been years ago.'

'What do you think happened to them?'

He shrugged into the night. 'Maybe they got caught. Maybe they went south. The sun is hotter in the south, and there's less people.'

Sophie said, 'How many do you think there are? How many rooftoppers?'

Gérard said, 'I would guess more than ten. Less than a hundred.' The girls nodded. Safi held out ten fingers and thumbs, closed her fists, opened them again. Anastasia said, 'I think that's right. About twenty or thirty. I see shadows, sometimes. I think there's probably someone living on the Louvre.'

They fell silent again. Two hours passed by. Sophie sat with her ears stretched wide.

No *gariers* appeared. There was no music. By five in the morning, Sophie was cold and tired enough to weep.

'We should go,' said Matteo. He knelt, and dusted off his backside. 'The sun's coming up.' He stood.

'Wait!' Gérard pulled him down. 'One second! Listen!'

'Cello?' Sophie snapped alert, and she balled her fists. '*Gariers?* Or music? Can you hear her?'

'No, neither. But listen.'

The rooftop was very still. Far away and down the road, there was a sound that might have been a horse, or someone coughing, or nothing at all. Then a cloud appeared; a grey cloud, which spun and zagged across the sky.

Anastasia breathed, 'Birds.'

Sophie said, 'Starlings.'

The air was suddenly thick with them. There were five hundred, a thousand. Their wings hummed, and they swooped down over the rooftoppers' heads as fearlessly as if the children were a cluster of chimney pots.

'They're like a ballet!' said Sophie.

'Maybe,' said Matteo. 'I don't know ballet. They're like starlings.'

'What do you call a group of starlings?' whispered Sophie.

'You call them starlings, don't you?' said Anastasia. 'I don't know what you mean?'

'Like, a flock of crows is called a murder. A group of owls is a parliament.'

'Oh. *Je comprends*. I don't know, though.'

'A ballet of starlings,' said Sophie.

They spoke without moving anything, not even their lips. The birds circled and dived. Each time they came near Sophie gasped: the others did not, but Sophie couldn't help it. It felt high-day-holiday miraculous. It felt like an omen. Her heart was hot, and enormous.

'An army of starlings,' said Matteo.

'A tornado of starlings,' said Gérard.

'An avalanche of starlings,' said Sophie.

'A fountain of starlings,' said Anastasia. 'A sunray of starlings.'

The boys snorted, but Sophie said, 'Yes! I like that. Or, an orchestra of starlings.'

'A rooftop of starlings,' said Matteo.

CHAPTER TWENTY-FOUR

They went home slowly. The roar of adrenalin had died away, and Sophie felt only exhausted. They went an unfamiliar route, single file, Matteo first and Safi last. Nobody wanted to talk.

Matteo and Sophie left the two sky-treaders and Gérard at the cathedral, and went north alone.

Once they were alone, Sophie said, 'Matteo? Just out of interest? What *do* you do about toilets?'

'Drainpipes,' he said. He did not elaborate.

Sophie laughed, and looked away. The surrounding buildings were becoming familiar. But – 'This isn't my

street, is it?' Sophie hesitated. 'Matteo? Where are we?'

He looked half asleep. 'Near the river.' He shook himself. 'It's a shortcut. Quite close to you, now. Ten more minutes.'

'But what building are we on?'

'The police headquarters. You should know that. You said you've been here twice.'

'And we're … on the roof?'

'Yes.' He looked confused. 'We're on the roof.'

'How long until sunrise?'

Matteo's mouth moved as he counted the remaining stars. 'Half an hour. Maybe forty minutes.'

'And the city archives are on the top floor of the police headquarters, aren't they?'

'I don't know.'

'Well, they are. I know they are. Could we … have a look? Just in through the window?'

'If you want.'

She laid a hand on his wrist to make him concentrate. 'How, though, do you think? How would you do it?'

'If you lie on your stomach and hang over the edge, I'll hold your legs.'

'And you won't … drop me?'

'You'll be fine.' Which was not, Sophie thought, exactly an answer. 'You just have to hope they don't have curtains.'

If he said she would be fine, she believed him. Sophie lay down near the edge and shuffled forwards on her stomach. 'Have you got me? Hold tight, won't you?'

Sophie shimmied forwards until her ribs were hanging over the edge of the rooftops. She gripped the brickwork and bent herself slowly forward, but she couldn't see in. The top window was some way below her. Sophie forced herself not to look down.

'A bit further,' she said. The blood was going to her head. 'A bit further!' It was no good. The window was too far down.

'Pull me up again,' she said. 'Quickly, please.'

Matteo gave a grunt, and tugged. Sophie's chin scraped against the brickwork as she rose. She sat up and rubbed it. Blood wetted her fingers. 'Damn,' she said.

Matteo pulled a scrap of cloth from his pocket. 'Spit on it,' he said. 'There'll be brick-grit in the scab if you don't.'

'Thank you,' said Sophie. She said it to Matteo's bottom, because he was peering over the edge. There was a pause, and then his feet started drumming on the rooftop. If feet can sound excited, Matteo's did.

He straightened up. 'You're right,' he said, 'it's too far to bend over. But what if I dangled you by your ankles?'

'What? No!'

'Why not? I'll hold tight, I swear. I'm strong.'

'By my ankles, though?' she said.

'How else? You said you wanted to see, didn't you?'

'I do.' Sophie's skin was suddenly itchy with terror.

It was like wearing a sandpaper suit. But it would be too terrible to give up now. 'All right,' she said. 'But make sure your hands don't get sweaty. I don't want to die upside down, thank you very much.'

She scooted forwards again, and Matteo took hold of her feet. His grip on her ankles was cutting off the blood supply. 'I'm going to lower you,' he said.

He pushed her forwards until only her knees could still feel the roof; then only her toes were touching the parapet. She could feel the muscles in his arms shaking, and she grasped the bricks for support. 'Don't look down,' she whispered. Her hair hung down over Paris. She shook it out of her eyes, and peered in the window.

The room stretched the length of the building. It was lined with filing cabinets. There must have been hundreds, for there wasn't a single gap. In the centre of the room there was a large table. She blew on the window, *hah*, upside down, and wiped the window clean with her fingertips. There were no pictures in the room, and no lights. Sophie's vision started to swim with red spots.

'I'm going to have to pull you up,' called Matteo's voice. 'Unless you want to take the fast way down.'

When all the blood in Sophie's body had returned to its proper place, the two went on, quicker now, for fear of the rising sun.

'The filing cabinets had locks on them,' she said. 'Do you think I could hammer them open?'

'*Non,*' said Matteo. 'The whole of Paris would hear you.'

'Damn. How else, though?' she said. 'Could I crowbar them?'

'But you pick the lock, of course.'

'How? Ouch!'

Sophie's nose met Matteo's foot. They were crawling over the peaked roof of a butcher's shop, and Matteo had stopped to stare at her.

'You've never picked a lock?' He sounded genuinely incredulous. 'I thought it was ... I don't know, like breathing. I thought everybody could.'

'Why would I know how to pick a lock?'

'Really? You really don't know? I can do it with my *teeth*.'

'For goodness sake, no, I don't!' They were in sight of Hotel Bost now.

Matteo stared at her. She felt herself turning red, and brushed her hair over her face to hide it. At last he said, 'I guess I'll teach you, then. It's easy. And it's useful. More useful than the cello.'

'When? Now?'

'*Non*. Your hands will be too stiff. You need to sleep first. Tomorrow.' He nodded towards the hotel. 'Can you do the last part on your own? I need to get home. The sun'll be up in ten minutes.'

'I'll see you tomorrow,' she said. 'And, Matteo –' She scrubbed at her eyes, to give herself time. It was difficult to think of the right words to thank him. But, when she opened her eyes, he had already vanished.

When Sophie dropped back into her room, the first strong sunbeams were warming her bed. The palms of her hands were black. There was soot and leaf mould all across the soles of her feet and up over her ankles.

The bed looked wonderfully inviting, but before she climbed into it she fetched the English dictionary from the bookshelf on the landing. She wiped her hands clean on the backs of her knees, and flicked through the pages.

A flock of starlings was called a murmuration.

CHAPTER TWENTY-FIVE

Sophie opened her eyes and saw Charles bending over her with a mug of something hot. Mid-afternoon sunlight streamed in through the skylight.

'You're back,' he said.

Sophie took the mug. She tried to look innocent. 'Back from where?' It was hot chocolate. It was rich and sticky, the way Charles made it at home. As a baby she had called it 'cocoa-extragavant'. It took half an hour to make it that particular, chewy thickness. Sophie's guilty feeling deepened.

'I don't know,' said Charles. 'You tell me.' He sat on

the bed. 'I came in at eleven last night and you were gone.'

'Was I?'

'I don't want to be a boring old fart, my darling, but I thought you'd been taken. I thought you had been ... I don't know.' He wasn't smiling, and there was no light in his eyes. 'Where were you?'

'I can't tell you.' She wrapped her fingers round his wrist. 'I'm so sorry. I would, honestly, but it involves people who aren't me.'

'Sophie, are you telling me –'

'But I promise, nobody could have seen me. I *swear*. I didn't go on the streets until it was dark. And I covered up my hair.'

'Why didn't you at least tell me you were going out?'

'I couldn't. I thought you might stop me.'

Charles took her mug from her, sipped, handed it back: all in silence. His eyebrows were raised so high they were almost on top of his head.

Sophie asked, '*Would* you have stopped me?'

'I wouldn't, no.'

'Oh!' Guilt caught at Sophie's chest.

'At least, I hope I wouldn't.' He took another draught from her mug. 'I might have. I don't know, actually. Love is unpredictable.'

Love is unpredictable, thought Sophie. She hesitated. Then, 'Charles? Can I ask you something?' she said.

'Of course. Always.'

Sophie tried to find the right words. To give herself time she gulped the rest of the chocolate, and ran her finger round the inside of the cup.

'It's only that I've been thinking – if she *is* alive – and I'm sure she is – why didn't she come for me?'

'But she would have been told you were dead, Sophie. If we couldn't get a list of survivors, neither could she. You wouldn't have been in the hospitals. Nobody in France would have known about you.'

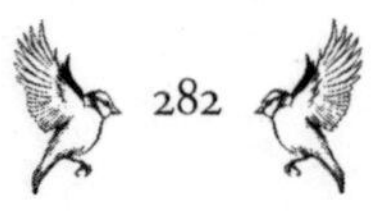

'I know. I do know that. But … they told *me* that *she* was dead, and I didn't believe them. Why did she believe it? Why didn't she keep looking?'

'My darling, because she is an adult.'

Sophie ducked behind her hair. Her face was hot and tight and angry. 'That's not a reason.'

'It is, my love. Adults are taught not to believe anything unless it is boring or ugly.'

'That's stupid of them,' she said.

'Sad, child, but not stupid. It is difficult to believe extraordinary things. It's a talent you have, Sophie. Don't lose it.'

CHAPTER TWENTY-SIX

That night, before Sophie climbed out of the skylight, she left a note for Charles on her pillow. It said that she was going to the police headquarters – though not that she was going via the sky – and it promised she would be back before dawn. Then she pulled on trousers, and Safi's grey rag of a jersey. She put a candle stump in her pocket, and flexed her fingers, and headed out into the dark.

Matteo was waiting for her on the roof, hopping from foot to foot. Sophie had expected that; but under the chimney stack sat Anastasia, Safi and Gérard,

passing round a bag of raisins. Both Safi and Anastasia were dressed in black jerseys and grey trousers, and their faces looked silvery-white in contrast. She had forgotten how beautiful they were. It gave her a shock.

Gérard saw her face and laughed. 'I know! *Mon Dieu, non*? But you get used to it, eventually.'

'We're here to keep watch,' said Anastasia. 'Gérard has hearing like a rabbit. He'll know if anyone's coming. And we brought food.' She tipped a dozen raisins on to Sophie's palm. As she ate them the sugar warmed her, and she turned to Matteo.

'Shall I go first?'

'*Non,*' said Matteo.

'No, but please. I'd like to.' It felt so important to do it right, but Sophie couldn't properly explain. She felt

she was so close. Every thought of her mother made her quiver.

Matteo said, 'Do you know how to break open a window latch?'

'Oh. I don't, no.'

'Then I go first.'

Matteo slid down a metre of drainpipe until he was level with the window sill. Sophie lay on her stomach and watched. She didn't want to say, 'Be careful!' She didn't want to be a 'be careful' sort of person. So she called, 'Good luck!' and after a second, unnecessarily, 'We'll keep watch!'

Matteo was facing the wall. Embracing the drainpipe with both arms, he swung one leg, then the other, to rest on the window sill, pressing his body flat against the brick. One hand let go of the drainpipe, and latched on to the brick. It made Sophie giddy to watch. Then the second hand swung across, and Matteo stood upright on the window sill, balanced on his toes. Slowly he bent his knees, gripping the window pane with his fingertips, until he was crouching. The window sill was

thick, but even so, his back half was sticking out over nothing. His face, though, was as calm as a Sunday afternoon.

He attacked the window latch with his penknife. 'It's open!'

'Good! Oh, please be –' Sophie caught herself just in time. 'Wonderful!' she called.

He hitched his nails under the sill and heaved. There was a ripping noise, and Matteo said, '*Ach.*'

'What? Are you all right?'

'Nothing. Just a little blood.' The window opened. 'We'll wipe it before we go.' He rearranged himself so that he was sitting on the sill with his legs dangling inside the room. 'OK!' He patted the sill. 'You can come down now.'

Sophie copied his movements as exactly as she could. Matteo guided her feet with both his hands. She forced herself to think of cellos, and mothers, and not of the noise her skull would make on the pavement if she fell. 'Mothers,' she whispered to herself. 'Mothers are worth hunting for.'

Sophie ducked in through the window. The archive room was chill and dark. It felt secretive, and wary. She said, 'Are you coming in?'

'*Non*. I never go inside.' Matteo kicked his heels against the wainscoting. 'I'll be fine like this.'

Sophie pulled the candle from her pocket and struck a match. 'Right.' She wrapped her hand in her jersey so that the wax wouldn't drip on her fingers. 'Where do I start?' She peered at the labels on the cabinets. 'Matteo, they're in French!'

'Of course they're in French. Read them out to me.'

'This one says, *meurtre*.'

'That's murders.'

'*Incendiaire?*'

'Firebombs. Probably not.'

She crossed to the far end of the room. '*Assurance?*'

'That's insurance. Try that one.'

Sophie tugged at the cabinet door. 'It's locked.'

She couldn't believe she had forgotten. But Matteo's face, framed in the window, was excited.

'Of course it's locked. Do you have a hairpin?'

'Yes.'

'Good. Now –'

'Wait a second.' Sophie fumbled at the pin holding back her coil of hair. Her fingers were shaking, and somehow fatter than usual.

'OK,' he said. '*Bon*. Now, you have to concentrate. A lock has *cinq* pins inside.'

'Sank?' It was the one word she was trying not to think. That, and 'drowned'.

'*Oui, cinq*. Oh! *Ach* … five. Numbers are ugly in English. A lock has five pins, *oui*? And the key moves the pins and opens the crossbar. Where's that match you used? Did you drop it on the floor?'

'No. It's here.'

'So, you put the match in at the base of the lock – like that, yes – and you push a little, left or right.'

Sophie licked her fingers to calm them, and inserted the match into the fat part of the keyhole. 'Which one?' she whispered. 'Left or right?'

'You can feel it. It's like water. It has a flow. One way is upstream.' Sophie wriggled the match. She couldn't feel anything.

Matteo said, 'Stop! You're trying too hard.'

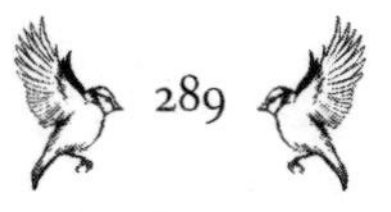

This is one of the most annoying things anybody can say. Sophie glared at him, her tongue still sticking out between her teeth. 'That's not terribly helpful, Matteo.'

'I mean, you're forcing it. You're poking it like it's a sausage. Imagine it's alive.'

'It's not.'

'How do you know? *Imagine* it is.'

And it was true. To the right, it stayed stiff; inched to the left, the lock gave a shift. It was soft as a whisper, and she repeated it a few times until she was sure.

'Now what?' she said.

'Hold it there. You mustn't move it a millimetre.'

'Right.' Sophie rearranged her grip so she could hold the match in place with her left hand. 'And now?'

'So, you push in the hairpin at the top of the lock.' He was watching her carefully, squinting through the dark. 'And you start at the back with the fifth pin. You slide the hairpin under it and you push upwards until it sticks.'

'How you do you mean, sticks?' Sophie's hands were

wet with sweat. She licked her palms, and dried them on her front.

'I don't know how to explain. It's easy. You just –'

'Couldn't you just come in and do it?'

'*Non*. But, you wriggle the pin until it feels … more solid. You just feel it. You hear a click, sometimes. But so quietly, if the lock is oiled. Like an ant coughing.' His mouth was slightly open, as though he were listening to music. 'That lock is oiled, I think.'

'And then?'

'Then you do the fourth pin, and the third. And then the –'

'Second, yes, I understand.'

'Can you feel the stick?'

At first, Sophie couldn't. She wriggled the hairpin up and down, feeling increasingly furious. And then, quite suddenly, she could feel it. It was the smallest possible shift, but suddenly the pin felt stiffer. It no longer wobbled.

'I think that's it! Now what?'

'Good. The first is the hardest. Now you pull the

hairpin towards you – less than a millimetre – and wriggle the next pin.'

Sophie held her breath, and pulled the hairpin back a hair's breadth. She made tiny digging movements with the hairpin to hitch it under the pin. It was easier, once she had got into a rhythm. 'That's the third,' she called. 'Second.' The final pin was the hardest. 'Done, I think!'

If she had expected congratulations, she would have been disappointed. Matteo gave a curt nod.

He said, 'Right. Now you keep hold of the hairpin – your hands are shaking, you must stop that – and you jerk the match to the left.'

The lock clicked open. Sophie hefted the file to the window and the two of them sifted through the papers. Sophie's fingers were quivering. It was hard to tell in the dim light, but she thought that Matteo's were too.

'There's nothing here on the *Queen Mary*,' she said. 'It's all from the last two years.'

'Don't worry,' said Matteo. 'We have time.'

'But there's thousands of files in this room!'

'We have time,' he said again. 'Don't panic.' His voice was more gentle than it usually was.

'Maybe I should try the older filing cabinets?' said Sophie. 'The green ones. They look rusty. They look less honest.'

He nodded. 'Put this back first, though. They mustn't know you were here.'

Sophie read the labels out to him. Pickpockets, theatre fires, beggars. But nothing that sounded promising.

'*Divers*,' she said. 'What's that?'

'It means "a jumble". Misc ... miscellaneous, you know? Try it.'

This lock was bigger, and the pins were easier to feel. It took Sophie and her hairpin less than five minutes to open it.

The files inside were fat, and the dates on the outside went back twenty years. Feverishly, Sophie found the right year. Then her whole body quivered and burned.

'*"Queen Mary", paquebot Anglais.*'

'What is *paquebot*?' she asked.

'I think – a large ship?'

The file was marbled cardboard; Sophie ran with it to Matteo's window sill, and handed him her candle. There were about two dozen sheets of paper, in all. She split them into two piles, and handed half to Matteo. 'Don't let them blow away,' she said.

Sophie flipped through the papers as fast as she could. There were printed lists of names, and handwritten letters. There were photographs of the waiters, staring unsmiling at the camera with napkins over their arms, and their names and addresses inked on the back.

'Ha!' cried Matteo. 'This is the passenger list, I think.'

Sophie took it from him. Under M, there was 'Maxim, Charles'. But there was nothing under V; no Vivienne Vert. She ran one shaking finger down the staff list with the same result. No Viviennes.

'Look!' said Matteo. He held up a photograph. 'Sophie! The band! Is she there?'

'Let me see!' Sophie almost tore it from his fingers.

'But …' she said. 'They're … they're all men.' The darkness in the room was suddenly terrible. 'The cellist is a man.'

'Oh,' said Matteo. His smile dropped downwards. 'Oh, *Dieu*.'

Sophie turned over the photo. 'It says the cellist is "George Greene, 12, Appartement G, rue de l'Espoir"'.

He was young and handsome, staring out at the world on the brink of laughter. He might just as well have been one-eyed and pot-bellied for all she cared. Sophie licked a tear off her nose. She hadn't realised she was crying. 'It's a man,' she said again.

'It's odd, though. Because George Greene looks very much like you,' said a voice.

Sophie nearly fell off the window ledge. A shadow was hanging from the drainpipe, watching.

'Move over, please,' said Safi. 'I want to sit down.'

Sophie ducked back into the archive room to make space on the sill for Safi. She gripped the girl's wrist. 'I don't see it. He doesn't! Does he?'

'He has your eyes,' said Safi. Her voice was deeper than Anastasia's, and more French. 'People never really

see their own eyes, so you wouldn't notice.' She turned to Matteo. 'I'm surprised *you* didn't see it, though. You talk about her eyes enough. Do you think it could be her father?'

Matteo flushed, but Sophie was busy looking at the picture. She held it up to the moon.

'My God,' she whispered.

A prickling started in Sophie's neck and ran down her back. She said, 'He's wearing a woman's shirt.'

'What?' said Matteo.

Sophie said, 'Women's shirts button right over left.'

'What?' said Matteo. 'How do you know that?'

'Of course I know. Buttons,' said Sophie, 'are important. Matteo, that's a woman's shirt. Why would a man wear a woman's shirt?'

'And,' said Safi, 'look at the shoes. Only women lace their shoes crossways, like that. See!'

Sophie did see. And she saw too that the trousers were black, and worn greyish at the knee.

'And,' said Sophie, 'look at his moustache!'

Matteo and Safi looked. 'What about it?'

'It's too short. It should come over the lip, surely?

Look at all the other moustaches. They're huge! But this is just the hairs that women have, painted darker.'

Safi took the photograph. 'I don't think that's a man,' she said. 'It's just a very clever woman.' She studied the picture, and then she reached out to Sophie, and pushed the hair away from her face. 'She looks like you.'

CHAPTER TWENTY-SEVEN

Sophie was still staring – at Matteo, at Safi, at the photograph – when there was a scuffle, and a thump, and a voice called from above their heads.

'Sophie? Are you down there?'

'Who's that?' said Safi.

Matteo said, 'The police! Run!'

Sophie gripped them both round the wrist. 'Wait! I think it's –'

'Would you mind coming back up?' said the voice. 'I have no doubt it's unintentional, but you are, metaphorically, scaring the hell out of me. Come back, please.'

It was Charles.

The three of them scrambled up the drainpipe. Matteo wiped a patch of blood off the sill with his elbow as he went, and slammed the window behind him. Sophie carried the photograph in her teeth.

Charles was leaning against the chimney pot, watched warily by Gérard and Anastasia. He held Sophie's cello in one hand, and his umbrella tucked under his arm.

'This young lady,' he said, pointing at Anastasia, 'very properly tried to kill me, until I explained I was your guardian. This young gentleman has convinced her I was harmless. I believe your cello convinced him.'

'You brought my cello?' Sophie stared blankly at him. 'Across the rooftops? How? Why?'

'I tied it to my back.' He looked ruminatively at the

cello. 'I rather thought you might need it, if you discovered something ... something grey.' He crouched down, and studied Sophie's eyes. 'From the look on your face, that is not the case.'

'I've got an address,' said Sophie. She was still shivering from head to foot. 'It might be her. I don't know.'

Matteo took the address from her. 'Rue de l'Espoir. That's *garier* country, near the church of Saint-Vincent-de-Paul. It's east of where we were last night.' The other three nodded.

'How do you know?' said Sophie.

Gérard shrugged. 'Rooftoppers have maps in their heads.'

Anastasia said, 'They'll be angry, Sophie. The *gariers*. Rue de l'Espoir ... that's like going into their front hall and singing Christmas carols.'

'I don't care,' said Sophie.

'You don't understand,' said Anastasia. 'Rue de l'Espoir is their headquarters. They carry knives.'

'You can stay here if you like. I'm going.'

Matteo said, 'Sophie, we never go there –'

'I don't care,' Sophie said again. She meant it. She had never felt less afraid. Perhaps, she thought, that's what love does. It's not there to make you feel special. It's to make you brave. It was like a ration pack in the desert, she thought, like a box of matches in a dark wood. Love and courage, thought Sophie: two words for the same thing. You didn't need the person to be there with you, even, perhaps. Just alive, somewhere. It was what her mother had always been. A place to put down her heart. A resting stop to recover her breath. A set of stars and maps.

Charles had been politely silent while the others were talking. Now he said, 'If we're going anywhere, Sophie, you and I should go at street level. I don't want to accidentally smash your cello on a chimney pot.'

'No,' said Sophie. 'I'm staying up here.'

'Why?' said Matteo. He was kicking at splinters of slate. His face was clenched tight.

'The police. If they caught me now ...' She didn't finish her sentence. Instead she said, 'Charles, I'll meet you there, all right?'

'No,' said Charles. 'That is very far from all right.'

She looked up at Charles. 'Please,' she said. Her gaze took in his long legs, and sharp bones, and the kindness of his eyes. 'I promise not to get hurt. You said to do extraordinary things. This counts as an extraordinary thing.'

Charles sighed. 'That is not untrue, perhaps.' He tried to raise his eyebrows, but they only flickered, and sank down. 'I can't think what Miss Eliot would say, but yes, that is certainly true.' His smile was strained. 'I suppose I will see you at rue de l'Espoir, then. If you're not there in an hour, I will … I don't know what I'll do. Just be careful.' He hitched the cello on to his back, and turned to the drainpipe.

'If you're going,' said Matteo, 'you'll need us. You don't know the way.'

'I know,' said Sophie. 'Yes. Thank you.'

Anastasia said, '*Mais, non!* Rue de l'Espoir –' She launched an angry stream of French at Matteo.

Sophie uncurled her spine. She had not realised how often she slouched. At full height, she was taller

than Anastasia, and almost as tall as Matteo. Sophie raised her eyebrows, and Anastasia and Matteo fell silent. 'You don't have to come,' she said. 'But if you're coming, let's go.'

CHAPTER TWENTY-EIGHT

They were twenty minutes past the river when Matteo's back began to tense. They were walking single file along the wide roof of a hospital, with Gérard bringing up the rear and humming to himself. They were going more slowly, more carefully than usual. Sophie and Matteo were in the lead, and she could see the hairs rising on the back of his neck.

'They've been here,' he said. 'Smell that? Tobacco.'

'Lots of people smoke tobacco,' said Sophie reasonably.

'But they smoke the butts of other people's. It has a twice-burned smell.'

'I can't smell anything. It just smells like chimneys to me. Can you, Anast –' Sophie turned. Anastasia was on the far side of the rooftop. Her face was yellow with terror. She was surrounded.

The boys had come noiselessly up the walls and across the neighbouring roof. They were tall, and pale. Their faces were arrogant, and sharp as acid. There were six; four of them had encircled Gérard. Nobody was moving.

Matteo backed towards Sophie. Sweat had flattened his hair against his face. He bent, snapped a piece of slate from the roof.

'They're angry,' he said. 'This was a bad idea.'

Nobody was laughing, nobody was jeering. The *gariers* held piping, broken shards of iron. *A wolf pack*, thought Sophie.

'Where's Safi?' she whispered.

Matteo shook his head. *'Je ne sais pas,'* he said. He pushed Sophie behind a chimney stack. 'Sophie, stay here. Don't move, or I'll kill you later, *d'accord*? And if Safi comes, hold her down, if you have to. You understand? Don't let her fight.'

Matteo pulled a pigeon bone from his pocket, and snapped it in half. The broken end formed a jagged edge, like glass. He handed half to Sophie. 'If they come for you, go for their eyes.' Matteo switched to French: he shouted something raw and bitter into the night, and then he hurled himself at the *gariers*.

The moon was covered and it was dark, but Sophie's eyes had grown accustomed to it. Sophie saw Anastasia catch sight of Matteo, and shout. She seemed to grow taller. One of the *gariers* had turned to meet Matteo, and Anastasia threw herself at the other. Anastasia didn't fight nicely. She hacked at his neck and chest with her nails, with her teeth. What terrified Sophie was how little noise was made. They fought in grunts and spits. Matteo saw Anastasia struggling, and he

pulled a chimney pot from the roof and threw it, straight at the back of the boy's head.

'It pays to know,' he panted, 'which ones are coming loose. Gérard, help me!'

Sophie understood, then, why they had called Gérard a fighter. His legs, which had looked so awkward on Notre Dame, were strong, and dangerous. He kicked two boys in the eye, raking at their faces with a flint held between his toes. But four to one are bad odds, and he was panting, and clutching at his left arm.

He called, 'Matteo!'

Matteo fought the way a cat fights. He darted in and out, aiming his shard of bone and his fists at the boys' eyes, their ears, their lips. In any playground, against any child, Matteo and Gérard would have won, but the *gariers* were not children. They were rooftoppers, and vicious. Gérard slipped, and hit the back of his head against the roof. One of the boys made as if to kick him in the face.

Sophie scrambled on the rooftop for a weapon. She had no idea if fighting was difficult, but sitting

crouched here was impossible. She jumped up and ran, head first, at the boy. He shouted and staggered, but he was up before she had wiped the dust and hair from her eyes. He stood over her, and she raised her knee and kicked him in the crotch. He groaned and collapsed.

Sophie retreated, and ducked behind the chimney pot again. As she watched, the tallest boy pulled a knife from his belt, a plain kitchen knife with a wooden handle. She used one like it at home to peel potatoes. He moved towards Anastasia. Sophie let out a noise that was half shriek and half roar. She jerked a slate from the roof, and threw it at the boy. It cut at his knuckles, and he swore and dropped the knife. Anastasia grabbed it, and dropped it down a chimney. The boy ran at Sophie. She gasped and tried to punch him, but swung at nothing. He spat something in French. She ducked his fist.

'He says, punch like you mean it,' said a voice.

Sophie turned, but she already knew it wasn't Matteo. A flat palm on her shoulder pushed her out of the

way, and Safi's fist connected with the bridge of the boy's nose. Blood spattered the rooftop.

'Kick him, if you can't punch him,' said Safi. Her voice was soft, but the expression on her face was not soft at all. 'Kicking is less personal.' Safi brought up a sharp knee, and slammed the heel of her hand into the boy's eye. 'You have to *mean* it.' He rolled to the ground, choking, and she vaulted over him.

'Where's Stasia?' said Safi.

'I'm here.' Anastasia scrambled towards them on hands and knees. 'Sophie! On your left!'

Sophie had always found it difficult under pressure to remember which was left and which right. Luckily, so did Anastasia. Sophie's hair was in her face and mouth and she kicked out blindly to the right, and felt her foot connect with a shin. Safi jerked an elbow at the boy's face as he went down.

There was only one *garier* standing now. Gérard was hunched over on the slate, coughing, and Matteo was leading the *garier* away from him. Matteo was white. He had a scrap of bone in each hand, but the

boy had a piece of pipe, and was backing Matteo towards the edge of the roof.

Safi took a stone from her pocket, squinted into the dark, and flung it. It hit the boy on the temple. He screamed and whipped round.

He saw the three girls standing, unblinking, in the night air. Two unconscious boys lay at their feet. Sophie whispered, 'Do not mess with a mother-hunter. Do not mess with rooftoppers.' She whispered, 'Do not underestimate children. Do not underestimate girls.'

The *garier* vaulted on to the next rooftop, turned, spat, and disappeared into the dark.

'Let's go,' said Matteo to Sophie. He was standing behind her. 'Quick. I don't want to be here when they wake up.'

'Are you sure? You can go back if you need to. I can go on alone.' The girls looked so fragile, now, in the moonlight. They looked like china dolls. 'Will you be safe?'

China dolls do not wipe their noses on their hair. Anastasia did so, and grinned. 'Come on, before it gets light. We'll be fine, Sophie. We're rooftoppers.'

CHAPTER TWENTY-NINE

Rue de l'Espoir was deserted. Charles was waiting, stamping his feet, in front of the apartment block. Sophie leaned over the edge of the building and whistled down to him.

'You were longer than I expected,' he said. Then he saw Gérard's bleeding temple, and Matteo's hands. He said nothing; only strapped the cello more securely to his back, and climbed up the drainpipe to join them.

They sat, the six of them, under the stars. It was a beautiful night, but it was too silent. There was not

a single cat, drunkard, or piece of litter. Sophie peered down at the street.

'Where is everybody?'

'There was cholera here; three times in four years,' said Gérard.

Anastasia added, 'That's why the *gariers* like it. Nobody will live here. People think it's cursed.'

Matteo snorted. 'People are stupid. Shall we break in to the apartment block?'

'No,' said Sophie. 'We'll call her.' Sophie cupped her hands to her mouth and then hesitated. What did she shout? '*Maman?*' she called. 'Mother?'

Matteo shook his head. 'Half the women in Paris are called *Maman*.'

'Vivienne?' called Sophie. 'Everybody, try together.

On three. One, two, three –' All six of them bellowed, '*Vivienne!*'

There was no answer, and no sound except the tin drum of Sophie's heart.

Charles handed her the cello. 'Here. Play the *Requiem*.'

'Why? Charles, I can't.' She felt awkward. To her surprise, the other rooftoppers were nodding.

'Play,' said Safi.

'Why, though?'

Anastasia said, 'Music will work the same way as magic does, sometimes.'

Matteo nodded. 'Only an idiot doesn't know that. Play, Sophie.'

Sophie had never been so nervous. Her heart had migrated down into her stomach, and her fingers felt thick on the strings. They were shaking. *Play*, she told herself. *Remember how it sounds when you dream*. The first notes were flat, and Gérard winced. Charles did not seem to notice.

'Yes!' he said. 'Quicker, Sophie!'

Sophie spat on the ground, and straightened her back. She played quicker.

'Louder!' said Matteo.

Anastasia kicked and spun on the spot. 'Quicker!' she called.

Sophie did not hear them. She played on, willing her fingers to go faster. *Come on*, she thought. *Please*.

When her arm ached too much to keep bowing, she stopped. Matteo clapped. Charles whistled. Safi and Anastasia whooped. The stars stopped spinning.

The music, though, kept going.

CHAPTER THIRTY

'Is that ... an echo?' Sophie looked round for Charles. 'Is it?' Her voice hurt her own ears. 'I can't hear it!' she cried. 'Has it stopped?'

It hadn't stopped. It had only grown fainter.

'It sounds like no echo I have heard,' said Charles. 'Echoes do not change key.'

It was Matteo who jerked them out of their shock. He shoved Sophie in the small of the back. She almost dropped her cello. 'Go! Now! *Vite! Mon Dieu*, are you deaf? Go!'

'Where's it coming from?' she said. '*Where? Quick!*'

'It's coming from the north-west,' said Anastasia.

She started to run, pulling Sophie along. 'Go west first.'

'Which way is west?' cried Sophie. 'Left or right?'

'Left!' said Safi. 'There, the roof with the black weathervane. Then the public baths; and then you have to jump.' Sophie turned and ran; Charles thundered after her. The slates under her feet cracked. The steps of the others faded.

'Sophie!' called Matteo. 'You're going too fast!'

Sophie was not, in her own opinion, going too fast. She was going not-fast-enough, and the music was swooping, as though to an end. She jumped two feet to the bathhouse; then there was a solid street's worth of pointed rooftops, and she ran, not bothering to keep low, along them. Anyone looking up would have seen a dark, soft-shoed blur.

'Sophie! Stop!'

Sophie came to a sudden halt. There was a side street between her rooftop and the next. The next rooftop was flat, but the gap was twice as long as her own body. It would be so great an anticlimax, to die now.

She stopped, choking on her own breath. She tried to prepare to jump, but her legs would not bend. 'I can't,' she whispered.

'You can.' Suddenly, Charles was behind her. 'I'll throw you across. Curl into a ball.'

She couldn't understand him. 'What?'

'Crouch!' He sounded like a sergeant major. Sophie crouched.

He said, 'Make sure to land on your feet and hands, not your knees. Knees are brittle. Not your knees, you understand, Sophie?'

Sophie nodded. 'Quick!' The music was fading.

'On three, Sophie. One. Two –' Charles hefted her in his arms, and swung her backwards. *'Three.'*

Sophie had not known that Charles was so strong. He had always looked spindly; but he lifted her with ease, and now the wind bit at her face, and then she

hit the opposite rooftop with a thud and felt the skin scrape off her palms.

There was another shout of 'Three!' and a thump. Matteo landed next to her.

'You! How did you get here?'

'I thought I'd catch you up,' he said. 'I didn't want to miss it.'

Then Charles jumped, with his legs outstretched, silhouetted against the street lamp. He landed on one knee, awkwardly, and brushed some dust out of his eyebrows. He spoke gruffly. 'I suggest, Sophie, that you don't mention this to the educational authorities. Throwing children across rooftops is frowned upon, I believe.'

Sophie stared at him.

'Go!' he cried.

Sophie ran on. Sometimes her panting covered the music and she thought it had stopped; but it kept playing, and always quicker, even when quicker should have been impossible.

Matteo was limping on his left foot, and she could hear him grunting in pain, but his face was steady.

Then Sophie heard Matteo gasp and turned back just in time to see his legs slip from under him. Charles was closer – he thrust his umbrella at Matteo as he slid, and Matteo grasped the hooked end. 'Hold tight,' said Charles. He tugged Matteo back up the slope, hauling hand over hand.

'You – are – more – substantial – than – you – look,' Charles grunted.

Using Charles like a stepladder, Matteo clambered to his feet. Charles must have seen how white the boy's face was, because he smiled through the strain. 'An Englishman without an umbrella is less than half a man,' he said.

Matteo stood, and as he did so a tile slipped down from under him and smashed in the street. Someone below shouted and pointed. Charles said, 'Speed would be ideal, here, I think.'

Sophie ran.

Music was not as easy to follow as she had imagined it would be; but surely, now, it was sharpening? It was coming from somewhere nearby. It was beautiful.

Then a voice, singing in French, was added to the music. Stars, Sophie told herself, do not sing, except in bad poetry; but, otherwise, she would have said the stars themselves were singing.

Sophie scrambled over the tip of a sloping roof, and stopped.

On the rooftop opposite, a single leap away, there was a woman. She sat with her back to Sophie. She sat on an upturned box, and she held the dark curve of a cello against her body.

Even in the dark, Sophie could see that the woman had hair the colour of lightning.

CHAPTER THIRTY-ONE

Sophie felt her heart physically shiver. 'Charles!' she cried. Her voice came out cracked and unfamiliar. She sounded starved. 'Charles! Is it her? Is that her?'

What if it wasn't her, she thought. She felt sick. What if it was?

'Go on, Sophie.' Charles pushed her forward, very gently. 'Carefully. Mind how you jump. We'll wait here.'

Sophie jumped. Her left knee cracked against the tiles as she landed, and a rivulet of blood ran ankle-wards. She ignored it.

She realised she hadn't thought about what she

would say. She had never got further than this in her imagination; but she would have to say something. What did you say? 'Good evening'? 'I love you'? 'What excellent weather'?

She need not have worried. The years of living with Charles meant Sophie stood upright as a weathervane and courteous as a cat as she walked towards the back of the cello player.

Sophie said, 'Excuse me?'

The playing continued. Sophie stepped a pace closer, and laid a trembling finger on the woman's arm. 'Excuse me,' said Sophie. 'Excuse me? *Bonsoir?* Excuse me.'

The playing stopped. The woman turned round.

Sophie said, 'Hello.' She swallowed. 'I'm ... I'm

hunting. I'm mother-hunting. I think you might be the thing I've been looking for.'

The moon shone down on them. The woman's eyes and nose and lips were Sophie's eyes and nose and lips. She smelt of resin, and roses. She had the sort of face, Sophie thought, that looked as if it had been around the world two dozen times. Her eyes were a colour that you do not expect to see outside of dreams.

Charles watched from the opposite rooftop. He saw the woman cry out; and then bend, and stare. He saw her kiss Sophie's ears and eyes and forehead; and then he saw the woman swing Sophie into her arms, and spin round and round until they looked less like two strangers and more like one single laughing body.

Charles squatted down against the chimney pots. 'Sit, Matteo.' He patted the rooftop beside him, and fished in his pocket for his pipe. It took two attempts to light – the first match was extinguished by the tears inexplicably running down his nose.

'Sit, come. Here, next to me. Have a puff of pipe. No? Let's leave them, for a little while.'

The music must have stopped, Charles knew, because the cello was lying on the rooftop, forgotten; but there seemed to be music still playing, somewhere, faster and faster, double time.

Another exciting adventure awaits!

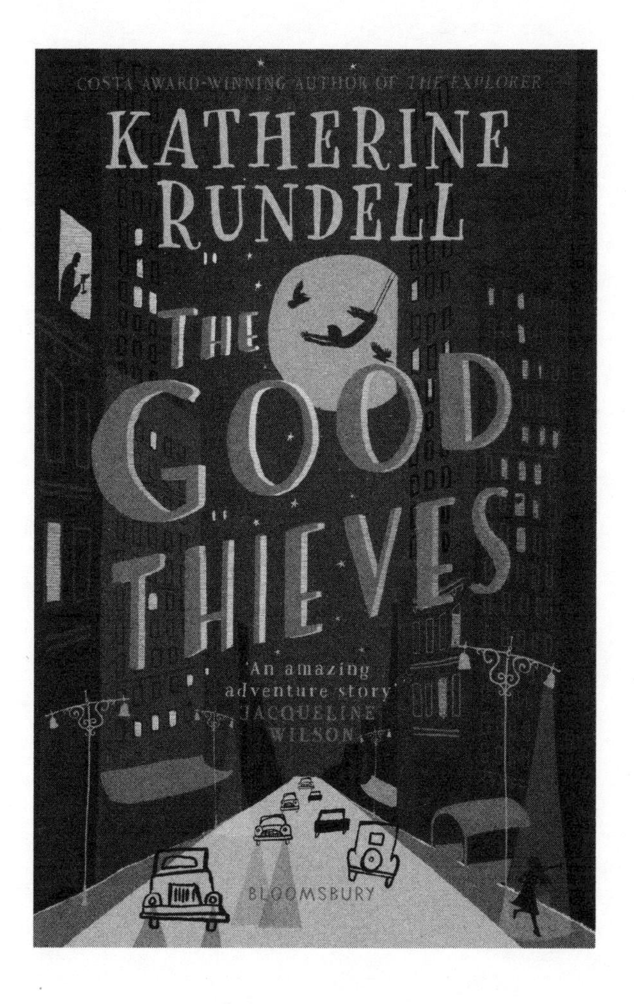

Read on for an extract …

CHAPTER ONE

Vita set her jaw and nodded at the city in greeting, as a boxer greets an opponent before a fight.

She stood alone on the deck of the ship. The sea was wild and stormy, casting salt spray thirty feet into the air, and all the other passengers on the ocean liner, including her mother, had taken sensible refuge in their cabins.

But it is not always sensible to be sensible.

Vita had slipped away and stood out in the open, gripping the rail with both hands as the boat crested a wave the size of an opera house. So it was that she alone had the first sight of the city.

'There she is!' called a deck hand. 'In the distance, port side!'

New York climbed out of the mist, tall and grey-blue and beautiful; so beautiful that it pulled Vita forwards to the bow of the boat to stare. She was leaning over the railing, as far out as she dared, when something came flying at her head.

She gasped and ducked low. A seagull was chasing a young crow across the sky, pecking at its back, wheeling and shrieking in mid-air. Vita frowned. It wasn't, she thought, a fair fight. She felt in her pocket, and her fingers closed on an emerald-green marble. She took aim, a brief and angry calculation of distance and angle, drew back her arm, and threw.

The marble caught the seagull on the exact centre of the back of its skull. The gull gave the scandalised cry of an angry duchess, and the crow spun in the air and sped back towards the skyscrapers of New York.

*

They took a cab from the docks. Vita's mother carefully counted out a handful of coins, and gave the driver the address. 'As close as we can get for that, please,' she said, and he took in her carefully mended hems and nodded.

Manhattan sped past outside the window, bright bursts of colour amid the storm-beaten brick and stone. They passed a cinema, its walls adorned with pictures of Greta Garbo, and a man selling hot lobster claws out of a cart. A tram thundered past at a crossroads, narrowly missing a van advertising *The Colonial Pickle Works*. Vita breathed in the city. She tried to memorise the layout of the streets, to build a map behind her eyes; she whispered the names: '*Washington Street, Greenwich Avenue.*'

When the money ran out, they walked. They went as fast as Vita could go in the ferocious wind, suitcases in hand, along Seventh Avenue, dodging pinstripe men and sharp-heeled women.

'There!' said Vita's mother. 'That's Grandpa's flat.'

The apartment building on the corner of Seventh and West 57th rose up, tall and stately in brown stone, from the busy pavement. A newspaper boy stood outside, roaring the headlines into the wind.

Across the road from the apartment block was a light-red-brick building, its facade arched and ornamented. Flagpoles protruded from its wall, and two flags flapped wildly. Above them, picked out in coloured glass, were the words 'Carnegie Hall'.

'It all looks very . . . smart,' said Vita. The apartment block appeared to purse its lips at the world. 'Are you *sure* this is the place?'

'I'm sure,' said her mother. 'He's on the top floor, right under the roof. It used to be the maid's apartment. It'll be a squeeze, but it's not for long.' Their return ticket was booked for three weeks' time. Enough time, said Vita's mother, to sort out Grandpa's papers, pack his few things, and persuade him to come home with them.

'Come on!' Her mother's voice sounded unnaturally bright. 'Let's go and find him.'

The lift was broken, so Vita half ran up the stairs to Grandpa's apartment, jerkily, as fast as her legs would take her. Her suitcase banged against the walls as she raced up narrow flights of stairs, ignoring the growing pain in her left foot. She came to rest, breathless, outside the door. She knocked, but there was no response.

Vita's mother came, panting, up the final flight of stairs. She bent to pick the apartment key from under the mat. She hesitated, looking down at her daughter. 'I'm sure he won't be as bad as we feared,' she said, 'but –'

'Mama! He's waiting!'

Her mother opened the door, and Vita went tearing down the hall; and then, in the doorway, she froze.

Grandpa had always been thin; handsome and lean, with long fine hands and shrewd blue-green eyes. Now he was gaunt, and his eyes had drawn back into his skull. His fingers had drawn inwards into fists, as if every part of him was pulling back from the world. A walking stick leaned against the wall next to his chair: he hadn't needed a walking stick before.

He had not seen her and, just for that second, his face looked sculpted from solid grief.

'Grandpa!' said Vita.

But then he turned, and his face was transfigured with light, and she could breathe again.

'Rapscallion!' He stood and Vita hurled herself into his arms, and he laughed, winded by the impact.

'Julia,' he said, as Vita's mother came in, 'I only got your telegram three days ago, or I would have stopped you –'

Vita's mother shook her head. 'Just try to hold us back, Dad.'

Grandpa turned to Vita. 'Smile again for me, Rapscallion?'

So she smiled, at first naturally, and then, when he didn't look away, wider, until it felt like every single one of her teeth was showing.

'Thank you, Rapscallion,' he said. 'You have your grandmother's smile, still.' Vita's stomach clenched as she saw tears rise up in her grandfather's eyes.

'Grandpa?'

He coughed, and smiled, and cleared his throat. 'God, it's good to see you. But there was no need.'

Julia pushed Vita towards the door. 'Go and find your room, darling,' she said.

'But –'

'Please,' said her mother. Her face was white, and exhausted. 'Now.'

'It's the one at the end of the corridor,' said Grandpa. 'More of a cupboard than a room, I'm afraid,' he said, 'but the view is very fine.'

Vita went slowly down the corridor, her suitcase in hand. She noticed how the floorboards squeaked; how the paint peeled from the wall. She pushed at the door. It stuck; she held on to the wall and kicked it with her stronger foot. It flew open, scattering thin shards of plaster.

The room was so small she could practically touch all four walls at once, but it had a wooden wardrobe, and a window looking out over the street. Vita sat on the bed, pulled off her left shoe, and took her foot in both hands. She dug her fingers into the sole, pointing and flexing the toes, and tried to think.

They had arrived. She should be thrilled. They had made it across the ocean, halfway around the world, and New York waited outside the window, stretching up to the sky like the calligraphy of a particularly flamboyant god.

But none of that mattered at all, because Grandpa wasn't as bad as she had feared. He was worse.

Vita's skirt pockets were full of gravel from the garden back home; she picked out the largest stones, and began to throw them at the wardrobe door. It helped her think.

A person watching might have noted that each hit the precise mathematical centre of the wardrobe handle – but nobody was watching, and Vita herself barely noticed. Her mind was not on the stones.

She had to do something to make it right. She did not yet know what, nor how, but love has a way of leaving people no choice.

Books to feed the imagination.
Go on an adventure with

KATHERINE RUNDELL

KATHERINE
RUNDELL
THE
GOOD
THIEVES
An amazing
adventure story
Costa award-winning author of The Explorer
KATHERINE
RUNDELL
'A writer with an utterly distinctive
voice and a wild imagination.'
Philip Pullman
ROOFTOPPERS

For younger readers

A gloriously illustrated story
that brings the magic of Christmas to life

For grown-up readers

An unmissable essay about
the importance of children's literature

ABOUT THE AUTHOR

Katherine Rundell is the bestselling author of five children's novels and has won the Costa Children's Book Award, the Blue Peter Book Award and the Waterstones Children's Book Prize amongst many others. Her novels are now published in thirty countries. Katherine spent her childhood in Africa and Europe before taking her degree at the University of Oxford and becoming a Fellow of All Souls College. As well as writing, she studies Renaissance literature and is learning, very slowly, to fly a small aeroplane.